The Gravedigger's Tale

Johannes T. Evans

The Gravedigger's Tale is a collation of nine short stories all with horror themes – several have been adapted from old posts of mine on the realistic-style subreddit, /r/NoSleep; several have been adapted from old TweetFics of mine; a few others are just scattered horror stories from my archives.

Letters from the Dead: 17k, rated M, first person POV. A few years removed – and thus safe – from his old posting, a gravedigger finally tells the tale of his haunting. Written in the style of a diarised blog post, originally posted on /r/NoSleep. CW for homophobia, grief, potential mental illness.

I Forgot My Manners: 2.7k, rated M, first person POV. A young woman forgets her manners when encountering strangers on the path, and lives in dread of the consequences. Written in the style of a diarised blog post, originally posted on /r/NoSleep. Set near to Llallwg National Park.

Wild Country: 3k, rated T, first person POV. A young woman walks home alone on a foggy night, and soon regrets it. Written in the style of a blog post, originally posted on /r/NoSleep.

The Door: 600w. They forgot about the door, somehow. Adapted from a TweetFic.

The Coffin at Sea: 400w. A vessel picks up a coffin afloat at sea. Adapted from a TweetFic.

The Ring: Rated T, 5k, M/M. A young man misses his departed boyfriend. Tragedy and horror and ghosts in this one — note CWs for different kinds of domestic violence implied throughout, infidelity, death and references to suicide and self-harm. Adapted from a TweetFic

Green Thumb: 2.6k, rated M. A chicken farmer tries to impress his new neighbour by growing him some flowers, but everything that he grows dies. Adapted from a TweetFic.

The Lighthouse: 700w. A ghost story.

The Shepherd: 1.3k. Abstract Horror. *Red sky at night, shepherd's delight.*

All stories included bar *The Shepherd* are set in my *Magic Beholden* universe, but are readable individually as standalone stories.

The Gravedigger's Tale is a work of fiction created from the author's imagination. Any resemblance to living persons, living or dead, or resemblance to actual events, places, or names is purely coincidental.

Letters from the Dead

Part 1

This story has been a long time in the making.

I've been meaning to write it down for years now, because it still… Well, I suppose to say that it haunts me is the wrong word, or maybe precisely the right one, but I've been meaning to write it down, and it's just never been the right time, or I've never been able to sit down and focus enough to do it.

Gez — Geraint, that is, my husband — has been on at me to write it down, though, has insisted that he wants to read it, because I've tried to tell him once or twice, but I've never been good at putting words together and talking out loud. I'm not too great at writing either, but I'm better at it than talking, I am, I swear.

And it needs to be told.

The longer I carry it with me, the heavier it feels.

My name is Ray, Ray Darvill, and these days I'm basically employed as my boyfriend's tech support, but for 19 years I was a postman, and for several years after that, I was a gravedigger.

In 2001, a few months after I'd turned forty, I was in a bad turnover on the M6. You might have seen about it in the papers at the time, I don't know if it was a big thing or not — I was on my way from the depot to my delivery rounds, and it was a pretty bad wreck. Some prick in a Saxo, on his phone and not watching the road in the pouring rain, rammed into me and sent me skidding into the path of an eighteen-tonne lorry.

I was in hospital for a while, but they cleared me up pretty well, and for all the pile-up it caused, I was mostly alright — no head injury, no damage to the spine.

Once they had me hopped up on morphine, the thing I was most worried about was the letters — my van doors had been busted open, and there was post all over the road in the pouring rain. Apparently, so the nurses told me, I was babbling like Hell about it.

I always wanted to be a postman when I was a little boy, you see, and I took it seriously.

After the accident, though, my hip was shot, always stiff — I ended up having a hip replacement a few years after the accident when it didn't improve. For the first few years, though, I limped quite badly, and I used a cane to get myself around. I could have stuck with the *Royal Mail*, could've taken a desk job, I s'pose, they did offer, but what I liked about it was the people, you know?

Not meaning to sound soppy about it, but I always thought letters were important, must've had about 20 pen pals when I was a lad, spent all my money on stamps, and whenever I went on my rounds, people'd know me, greet me, and they'd be pleased to see me. Who isn't happy to see their postman?

Well. People with big bills, or pushy mothers, or whatever else — but the majority of people were pleased to see me, enjoyed the routine of me, and I was pleased to see them.

I didn't want to sit at a desk and do admin in the depot. It wasn't what I'd signed up for.

I went back to my home town, a village in the south of England — forgive me if I don't say which one, but you'd be able to figure it out anyway, once you have all the details — and I took my granddad's old bungalow.

My parents wanted me to be closer to them, because they'd been in pieces at me being alone in the hospital and then in my flat, being as I was at the time a *confirmed bachelor,* as my granddad would've called it, and to be honest, I wanted to be closer to them, too. They were getting on a bit, and I'd had a bad scare — and they'd never actually been fussy about me being gay, you know, just until I met Gez, they were concerned I was so bad at it, and didn't like me being alone.

So I packed up my stuff and my cat — fat, lazy little twat called Wodehouse, who's still alive, don't worry about that, although he's 22 now and all the lazier for it — and I came home.

I'd been in contact with the man at our old church: Arthur, his name was, and we called him Pastor Arthur. He was in his mid-seventies in '01, and although he was sprightly for his age, he was getting on a bit in years.

My granddad, when he was alive, also called Ray — although everyone used to call him Raymond — had been the gravedigger at the little chapel for the big village cemetery, which was across the field from the proper church.

They only really used the chapel for funerals, and the bungalow was just around the corner from it — it was a nice little building built in the late 1800s, with a mausoleum sort of half-underground, and even its own bell tower. When I was a little boy, I used to walk out there on Friday afternoons and meet my granddad after school, and I'd sit in his office as he did clerical stuff and whatnot, and I'd walk home with him to have tea, me, him, and my granny.

"They don't call it being a gravedigger anymore, of course, but a *cemetery worker*," Arthur said to me as I came into chapel, and I watched the old man's eyes zip down to my bad hip and the way I was leaning my weight on my cane, "and you wouldn't have to dig any graves. We get a third party to do that, anyway — they've a digger for that these days, and they measure out the plots and such. It's... Can I be frank with you, Ray?"

"'Course, Pastor," I said. "You're the one offering me a job."

"You don't have to take it if you don't want," the old man said, folding his ancient hands loosely over his belly and looking at me seriously. It was funny, seeing him in a cardigan and a shirt — when I was little, I'd only ever seen him in his vestments, and without them on, he seemed half the size. "We get all these young kids, nineteen and twenty, who take the job for a year, and none of them have any sense of organisation. Perfectly pleasant young people of course," he added hurriedly, in his affable way. "But perhaps slapdash."

I chose not to mention at the time the fact that I could smell the lingering scent of weed as we went back into my grandfather's old office.

"The chapel's on a shortlist, you see," the pastor said. "In the new year, the Beeb want to film a documentary here, you know — not just here, of course, they're going into a lot of old chapels built around the same time period, and even if they weren't, I just... Your grandfather used to run a tight ship, you know that. Perfect files, everything in its place, everything quick and done to perfection. This..."

He and I stood together in the middle of what had once been my grandfather's office, and we looked at the old chapel, the newspapers and half-finished paperwork scattered around on every surface, the half-filled ashtrays, and a bouquet of flowers wilting in the windowsill.

"You want someone you don't have to supervise," I said, and the old man looked at me powerlessly.

"I don't have time, Ray," he said. "And you know, I know I'm asking a lot of you, and if you're not actually looking for work— "

"I'm not put off," I said. "This'll do me, Pastor — help an old friend, keep myself busy. So long as my leg's not a problem."

"The benefit of our dearly departed, Ray, is that they rarely require us to give chase," he said. "I think you'll be safe."

I laughed at that.

"Show me how to do the forms," I said, "tell me what I can do to help. Save you having to do another job interview."

"Oh, good," he said, sagging with relief, and he put one of his wizened hands on my shoulder. "You know, Ray, I *hate* job interviews."

***

I'd helped my grandfather out when I was a young lad — I used to trail after him until I was eleven or so, follow him about and linger in the background as he did what he did, and then when I came to visit my grandparents when I was a teenager, and my grandfather was starting to get on a bit, I used to dig a few of the graves with him, and I'd help trim the hedges, take care of the rose garden, and all that.

He used to be so gentle with the bereaved, I remembered that.

He didn't talk much to them, really, but he was a big man, with comforting way about him — d'you know the sort of men that are big, but hold themselves so that they're smaller? A teddy bear, my granny used to call him — a big, heavy bloke, but cuddly.

I was relieved, when I realised how little of that part of the job I actually had to do. There was a company who did the graves, dug them and filled them again, and even did the big hedges that went all around the graveyard edges. What I was to do was to keep on top of the more minor bits of horticulture, make sure the graves were kept in good condition, and mostly, fix up the inside of the chapel.

It hadn't been used for funerals in a few years, Arthur explained to me, and they'd just been using the file room and the office — there was dust and cobwebs all over the short pews, more like benches than pews, really, and a lot of extra chairs and fold-out tables for the village fête were stored in here to keep them out of the way.

The chapel had a small central hall, with a raised stage at the front underneath a stained-glass window of Saint George that was in surprisingly good nick compared to everything else, although the altar that I remembered being there when I was a kid had apparently been smashed by some teens who'd broken in a few years back, and been taken out.

In the wings of the chapel, on one side there was a records room, which kept records for the whole parish from since the chapel had been built, and underneath, an old mausoleum, with some inset graves that were all from 1860, or something like that. The mausoleum was half underground, but you could see its roof from the outside, albeit overgrown with ivy that crept up the walls and roof of the old building.

It's insidious stuff, ivy — once it really makes itself at home, it's hard to tug it loose without ripping out any of the cement.

In the other wing was the gravedigger's — the *cemetery worker's* — office, and past that, there was a door into the base of the old bell-tower.

"The bell doesn't work, does it?" I asked on our first little tour of the building. "I remember it never rang."

"Well, I'm sure it's a bit rusted, but the bell should be in good condition," Arthur said, and he took the key to the bell tower, which was noticeably more old-fashioned than the others on the gravedigger's set of keys, and he gently pushed open the door to the tower's bottom. It wasn't a very tall tower — only a little bit taller than a house — but it was further than you could get up to without stairs, of which there were none.

"This used to have stone stairs, but shrapnel came through that window," Arthur pointed to the big window, which was plain frosted glass, without any stained design like most of the other chapel windows had, "during the war, and knocked out the main stairs. It was lucky there was no damage done to the rest of the chapel, really. They replaced it with a wooden frame for a long while, but it started to rot in the fifties. One of the younger bellringers fell when the first landing gave way, poor lad, and we stripped out a lot of the old stairs. We always meant to have it replaced, but we just never had the money, or the time."

I nodded my head, looking up toward the top of the tower, where a splintering stair showed just underneath a closed hatch, the last remnant of whatever ladder had once been there.

"Was the bellringer okay?" I asked.

"Oh, yeah, in the end," Arthur said. "Your grandfather called for a doctor — all he had was a nasty knock on the head and a sprained wrist, but Raymond, he took safety very seriously. I sometimes get annoyed at some of the risk assessment stuff we have to do, but I think about how well he'd look on it, from time to time."

I smiled. "Safety's important," I murmured.

"Yes," Arthur agreed. "But your gramps, I hope you don't mind me saying, was a bit of a scaremonger."

I remembered the old man's warnings for everything I did — making sure a ladder was steady, keeping my eyes on the road and both hands on the wheel when I was driving, checking the light was off twelve times before checking the switch off. I'd babbled on about that in the hospital and all, the nurses had said, what my gramps would say about that prick in his Saxo, who'd come out of the accident with not even a scratch.

"Yeah," I said. "I miss it, sometimes."

My grandfather had died in '92, about a decade before all this, and Arthur had sighed, and nodded his head.

"Me too," he said, and then we walked back into the office to go over how the paperwork was done, what needed to be recorded, what he wanted kept from all the stuff in the office.

"I'll leave you to it," he said then. "Give me a ring if you need anything else."

"Will do," I said, and got to work.

For the first few weeks, I set myself into a regular routine.

I tended to work a sort of loose eight to six — I'd come in in the morning, meet up with the young lad, Joel, who worked with the digging company, and walk through the grave plots with him for the week, take in the forms that needed doing, make sure it was all sorted out. None of it was complicated paperwork – most of it was just checking off which graves had been dug and emptied, cleaning and tidying, some risk assessments, double-checking funeral or burial arrangements, and checking with families or funeral homes about headstones or other grave makers.

Joel actually offered when he first met me to do the mowing for me, what with my leg, and said he'd been doing it the past few weeks anyway, and I wasn't exactly going to turn that down — I fucking hated mowing grass even before I lost a game of head-to-head with a lorry.

I'd do two rounds of the cemetery a day — once when I came in in the morning, and once before I went home in the evening, and when I walked out to the bungalow for lunch in the early afternoon, I'd keep a casual eye out.

There wasn't much that needed to be inspected, really — when flowers were really on the way out and withered, after a week or longer on the gravesite, I'd take them away, but other stuff I'd normally leave in place. I've heard tales of teens messing about in graveyards, but I never had a problem with it the whole time I did that job, except for the story about the altar, and that had happened when I'd barely been old enough to walk.

A few people walked their dogs through the cemetery, but that wasn't disrespectful in itself — the only thing that bothered me about it was when they let their dogs off the leash and let them run all about, and then I'd ask people to maybe keep them in a bit closer, but no one ever kicked up a fuss.

Most of my job was spent inside, cleaning up the chapel.

I made up a list, to begin with, of everything as needed doing —clearing cobwebs and dust and cleaning in every room, inventory that needed doing on the tool shed, maintenance on the guttering, ivy that needed cutting back from the windows, a few light bulbs that needed changing, and so on, but that would come later.

To begin with, I started on the office.

I tossed out all the ashtrays and the rubbish first, and then I started to sort all of the clerical work that had been neglected, fixing the stuff that was ingoing and outgoing, the checks and forms that were out of date and the stuff that still needed to be completed. Apparently, the last person who'd worked the job, a young woman in her twenties, had gone on holiday to Ibiza and never come back, and this was the state she'd left it in.

Funnily enough, I think it was the sort of work I really needed at the time.

It was quiet, meditative, just sorting and organising and stacking things to be attended to without being cooped behind a desk, and every day I'd work out a schedule for myself.

When I got up for breakfast, Wodehouse would be waiting for food; I'd do a round of the cemetery, do paperwork, go home and join Wodehouse for lunch; I'd go back to the paperwork, do one last round of the cemetery, and then I'd drop in on my parents, or go into the pub.

Everyone knew me as Raymond's grandson, and they were nice enough, chatted in the pub or in the shop — people were a bit funny about my leg, tended to stare at the cane but didn't want to ask about it, but they weren't any funnier about that than they were asking why I wasn't married.

It was nice, is what I'm saying, and I didn't feel depressed, really, or anything like that, that's important for you to know — I was sad I wasn't working as a postman any longer, but I wasn't having a breakdown over it, you know? I was just doing a job, and living quietly.

If I'd been having a tough time, if I'd been struggling, or if I'd been depressed, maybe I'd have thought I was hearing things, but I felt fine, felt, you know, alright, so that's not what I thought.

I first heard it when I was in the office, and I was on my hands and knees, cleaning out the old fireplace — there had been a board in front of it, and a few of those file boxes stacked up in front of it. All the people who'd been using the office the past few years, it seemed, had been using this battered old halogen heater that ambled around on three out of four squeaky little wheels, but I like a fire place, and I remembered learning how to put a fire together when I was first in this office, kneeling on the rug beside my granddad as he showed me the coal and the firelighters.

The whispering was so loud, I almost thought someone had somehow snuck in right behind me, but when I turned around, there was no one there. I could still hear them, though — two hushed voices speaking quietly to themselves, and then the sound of laughter, like two young men sharing a joke.

Just like that, it was silent again.

I can't quite remember what I thought about it — I suppose I put it down to the sound having travelled down the chimney from outside, or something like that. I remember I heard the sound very clearly, and I remember taking note of it and thinking it was strange, but it didn't linger with me at first. I didn't puzzle over it, you know.

But that was the start of it.

The next time that there was something strange — this time, something frightening — it was on a Thursday evening, and it was a little past seven o'clock.

It was November, and I'd been scrubbing some of the benches in the main chapel, working some of the grime out of them. I'd been alternating between doing that and doing some of the backdated paperwork, so that I didn't have to spend too much time sat low down, to keep the strain on my bad hip to a minimum. The cold weather was making it ache worse than usual, and it was almost always stiff. I had these exercises I was meant to do, but honestly, I rarely ever did them at the time — the only reason I do my exercises these days is because Gez does them with me.

Because I'd gotten so into the work, more time had passed than I had expected, and I did my rounds of the cemetery later in the evening that I ordinarily would. I sort of rushed about the yard with my cane, limping away, and had my lantern in the other hand — I had a proper torch on a carabiner on my belt, but I liked the lantern because it was a wind-up camping thing, and it let out a really wide range of light all around me. It wasn't as bright as the torch was, but it gave me a more complete view of things, even if it probably did look stupid like something out of a ghost story, me limping along with my lantern held aloft.

But because the light wasn't very bright, it didn't stretch all that *far* ahead of me.

Ahead of me on the path, as I went to leave, I saw a silhouette of a man I hadn't seen before — or at least, I didn't think I had. I couldn't really make out much about him — I saw that he was skinny and that he was looking down at a grave, but I couldn't really make out anything about his face or what clothes he was wearing.

He wasn't a regular visitor to the graveyard that I'd seen before, though, and as I limped further up the path, I said — gently, I wasn't being a prick about it — "Excuse me, sir? I was about to lock the side gates as I left, but you'll still be able to go out of the main one."

I thought it was weird that he didn't turn his head, and then...

Well.

I lifted my lantern higher, to try to see him better, and he wasn't there anymore.

There was no sound of him running away, no sudden movement, nothing — a silhouette of a man had been ahead of me a second ago, and suddenly, he wasn't any longer.

I'll admit it freely: it spooked me.

Sent a shiver down my spine, it did, and I very quickly limped to the side gate to lock it. I felt cold and shuddery, feeling all my hairs stand on end, and I tried my best to shake it off as I went back to the chapel to lock up, then realised the lights were on inside.

They hadn't been on as I'd left — I hadn't locked the doors just yet, because I'd left my satchel just inside the door so I didn't have to carry it around the yard with me, but I'd turned off all the lights. I was sure I had — and yet when I pushed the door open, the main chapel lights were on, and more than that, the lights in the corridors were on, the lights in the office, in the file room, even.

I went around to turn them all off, and I don't know what it was that made me check, but it was just a funny sort of tug at the base of my belly — maybe I told myself it must have been something to do with the fuse box, lighting all the lights at once, I don't know. But I took the big heavy key for the bell tower, unlocked the door, and pushed the door open.

When I saw the lights in there were on too, it was exactly what I expected to see and also punched me in the gut, both at once.

I quickly shut the light off, dragging the door fast shut behind me and locking it again, and then I went into the office to check nothing had been touched, and it didn't seem to me that anything had been, but...

Maybe this has happened to you — have you ever been looking for something, your wallet or your phone, and you've put it down somewhere, and you go through the whole house looking for it, checking everywhere, and it's absolutely nowhere to be found?

But then you walk into a room you've already checked three times, and suddenly, it seems almost as if someone's circled it for you — it's the first thing your eyes jump to, and it was somewhere obvious the whole time, and you think you were an idiot for never seeing it before?

I had a moment like that.

Standing in the doorway of my office, I stared dumbly at the fireplace that I'd spent the past week cleaning out to work on, and realised that one of the bricks was loose.

The bricks were grey, such a light hue they were almost the same colour as the cement that had glued them into place, and I moved slowly forward, staring down at the brick I'd suddenly noticed, and somehow never noticed before. I could see the gap in the cement, see the dark shadow where the brick was loose, and very slowly, still trying to shake off the willies I was feeling, I reached out and tugged it loose.

I don't know what I expected — for some sort of monster to jump out of the gap and bite my fingers off? See a gremlin or a ghost or what have you? Maybe, I don't know.

None of that happened, anyway.

There was a puff of old stone dust that made me cough, but inside, there were no little monsters that I could see — there was a tin lockbox, blue but caked with the cement dust, and I had to lean my cane against the chair to use both hands to pry it out, and when it fell and hit the tile with a loud clatter, I almost pissed myself, let me tell you.

I tugged the little lockbox free, and I expected it to, you know, actually be locked, but it wasn't.

I opened it up, and stacked tightly, bound with yellowing twine, was a stack of envelopes — the paper of the envelopes was turning yellow too, and it looked old, *very* old. There was no date or address on them — they all said the same thing, in a spidery, looping handwriting — and that was old-fashioned, too.

"Peter," I said aloud, reading the name written on the envelope: at the exact same time, a voice whispered in my ear, loudly, with breath so cold I felt like an icy wind had done it, *"Dear Peter."*

It shocked me so hard I jolted, shifting my weight so that my bad side buckled, and I cried out as I hit the floor on my side, swearing at the top of my lungs for the pain as I looked wildly around for whoever was there, but there was no one.

With shaking hands, I reached for envelopes and I picked them up again, turning them over, looking for a sign of a date or an address on any of the envelopes further in the stack, but there was nothing there. Every envelope just had the same name written on it in the same cramped handwriting: *Peter*.

I was shaken, and I quickly put the letters back into the lockbox, and limped back to the entrance of the chapel, dropping the lockbox into my satchel, and then I turned off the last of the lights and locked the chapel behind me before I made my way home.

I didn't open the letters up right away.

That night, I went back home to my grandparents' old bungalow, and I checked that the front and back doors were locked twice,

Wodehouse tubbily winding his way around my ankles the whole time, before I even took a breath to put the kettle on.

Once the beast was fed, he agreed to act as my bodyguard, and sat his huge arse on the arm of my granny's old chair as I sat back in it with the TV on for the sake of the noise — Wodehouse had come to terms quite quickly with the fact that I complained if he sat his fat weight on top of my thighs after my accident, but he would always sit next to me like a round gargoyle when we watched TV together.

I fell asleep to the sound of his purring.

It was the last peaceful night's sleep I'd have for a while.

Sorry, I need to take a break — speaking of the pudgy old prick, Wodehouse is currently screaming up at me from the floor, and advising me it's time for his supper before Gez and I go to bed. He never asks Gez for food — always pesters me, instead. I think it's because Gez has been putting him on a diet, or trying to.

I'll be back with the next part soon.

Part 2

I was having the dreams again last night, stronger than before. I woke up a few times, almost crawled out of bed and back to the computer to keep writing it all down, but Gez sleeps on top of me like I'm his personal bloody pillow, and he was wrapped around me last night — maybe he knew I was having nightmares, I don't know.

He hasn't mentioned it this morning, but he never does. He knows I don't want to talk about it, I s'pose, and I did say I was writing it down.

It's a little past seven, and he's in his office on the other side of the village — he's a counsellor, and he prefers to do everything in his little office, and there's no one else in there with him, so he doesn't have to worry too much about Covid restrictions. All the appointments he does are via video.

I'm waffling — procrastinating, I guess. Avoidance and all that.

The nightmares are relevant, though. I had my first of the nightmares the night I took them letters home.

I don't normally dream much. Not that I never dream, you know, but I just don't dream very often — or if I do, I almost always forget them.

The dream sort of started out where I thought I'd woken up — I was sat up in the armchair and came to, and Wodehouse was gone, and somehow, the TV had turned off. I sat there for a moment, thinking that something had woken me up, but I wasn't sure what, and then, it was like...

It was like being assaulted with sound.

I could hear lots of sounds all at once and I could pick them out of the cacophony (looked that up in the dictionary, no harm in that), but they were all happening at the same time, painfully loud: pages turning and voices talking sort of whispered and hushed and a knock on a door and screaming and a bell ringing and splintering wood and a big clatter of something hitting a tiled surface and trees creaking in the wind and the wind itself howling up a storm and everything else—

I put my hands over my ears and screamed and shouted for it to stop, because it felt like all those sounds were advancing on me, like somehow they were solid and I was going to be crushed between them all, and then it went so silent I thought I'd gone deaf.

It was the shock of the silence that woke me up properly, and when I blinked awake, I had a crick in my neck I'd not had in the dream, and Wodehouse had sort of strangely worked himself into my armpit like a hot water bottle so I was soaked with sweat on one side more than the other, and the television was flashing brightly as *Dad's Army* played on mute, so I turned it off.

I hadn't put it on mute myself, but given that the picture was also scuppered, I put that down to Wodehouse stepping on the remote rather than any ghostly intervention — he had an awful habit of doing that. Still does now.

I was shivering a bit, still in my work clothes and, as I said, damp with sweat, and it was still dark as anything, but it was about five o'clock, or something like that. All the lights were still on in the house, and I felt silly about it, about my turn the night before, and I almost turned a few of them off, the ones that didn't need to be on, but I just didn't. I even reached out for the light switch in the corridor to switch it off, because the light in the living room always lit the little corridor just fine, but I was cowardly about it, and pulled my hand back.

I turned on the hot water and had a shower, and spent far longer under the spray than I really needed to — my parents had kept my grandfather's bungalow in pretty good nick since he died. He'd died in '92, and my grandmother had died a few years before, and although my parents had given away some of their personal effects, not the photos, you know, but knick-knacks and what-have-you, they'd left most of the furniture and the sheets and stuff, so that when any family wanted to visit, they could stay in the bungalow, and they'd never sold it — I think, really, because they wanted me to come home and live nearby. Not under the circumstances I did, obviously, but I think that was why they'd never sold it on.

Anyway, my granddad had been getting on a bit before he died, and although he always kept at his job in the graveyard, he had a few things put in the house that I used then — there were bars to help you get in and out of the bath, which is a godsend when you've got one weak side and can't trust the purchase you can get even on the shower mat, and he had this brilliant, white plastic shower chair with a sort of plastic cushion on it.

Me and Gez don't live in the bungalow — we rent it out to some funny, artsy looking girl with an Irish Wolfhound — but I brought that chair with me, and Gez hates it, is always wrestling with it when he wants to shower himself.

That morning, I sat on that chair for ages — I barely even scrubbed myself down, just sort of sat under the water and tried to rub the ache out of my neck, and did my best to make sense of the night before.

I just kept thinking about the man I'd seen in the graveyard and how he'd disappeared like a puff of smoke, and how I couldn't think of what he looked like, because I'd not really seen him properly, you know? I sort of sat there, my head in my hands and my elbows on my knees under the shower, and I tried to think of everyone I knew in the village and slotted them into the silhouette I'd seen and tried to make them fit, but no one did.

I didn't even really remember the actual letters until the water started to go cold and I had to get out — I remembered getting them out, and I remembered the scare I got in the chapel, but I forgot that I took them home until I stepped onto the bathmat, and then I remembered all at once, and I felt a sort of cold, horrible dread take hold of me.

I couldn't think why I'd done it as I dried myself off and put on fresh clothes — it seemed mad to me, like the actions of someone else. Why the fuck had I decided to bring them home?

I should have left them there.

I should've put them back into that loose brick and pretended like I'd never laid eyes on it, but that wasn't what I'd done, and now I'd brought them cursed letters home and put them in my *house*.

I went into the little kitchen in a daze, put a tin of food out for Wodehouse, and put some sausages in the frying pan to cook, and after I'd drunk a little bit of my tea, I sort of looked at my satchel out of the corner of my eye, like it was a girl I was trying not to make eye contact with in a club, in case she got the wrong idea.

When I opened it, I think I was hoping it would be gone, or that I'd dreamed it up, but obviously, I hadn't. There was grey stone dust all over the inside of my satchel off it, and I slowly lifted it out, and put it down on the little kitchen table.

Wodehouse, mistakenly thinking it might be more food — he'd already finished his finest from the supermarket — toddled up and gave it a cursory sniff. I stood there, holding my breath, waiting for him to hiss or yowl or stand up on his back paws and make the sign of the cross or something.

He just dropped heavily onto his back and made the table creak, although it did make me laugh, so I was grateful for that.

I didn't read all the letters at once, so I suppose what I'll do is sort of transcribe them — I still have them, normally keep them in the back of the wardrobe in that same box, although much cleaner now — one by one, but at the same time as I read them myself.

They weren't dated or nothing, like I said before — they were just in a kind of sheaf tied together, and now I smelled them in my kitchen, instead of in the chapel where it had smelt of stone dust and soap and still a bit of fag smoke, they smelled musty, like old paper did, and a bit waxy, like they'd been sealed with it, but when I pulled the first envelope out of the stack, I could see it hadn't been sealed at all — none of them had.

The tongue of the envelope had just been folded into the opening, and the glue was very dry and felt rough under my fingers when I touched it — it had never been wetted.

I've never been a psychic or believed in any of that shite, but stood there in my kitchen, holding that envelope in my hand, I felt the sort of... I felt an absolute, real *certainty*, knew it right down to my bones, that no one had ever opened it before.

It's not right to read someone else's post — my grandparents, both of them, always nailed that into me, even before I ever thought about being a postman. They got sent other people's post sometimes, because there was another Ray Darvill but spelt with an E — Darville — who was a farmer, and whenever my gramps got the post misdelivered, he'd put the envelopes in my satchel and pat me on the head and send me to walk out to the Darvilles and give it over.

I think I asked him once, if he wasn't ever curious what got told to Mr Darville in his letters, and he went off on a whole speech about how morally wrong and reprehensible and all that that it'd be to open someone else's post, 'cause it was an invasion of privacy and you could get hauled in by the coppers and all that.

It didn't occur to me then, though, that my grandfather had ever seen the letters. The lockbox was old enough, and made of tin without plastic, and it was very square — it could easily have been in that wall long before my granddad took up his shovel and the job.

My instinct was to return the letter to sender, but there wasn't even a delivery address, let alone an RTS, and as I sort of worked my finger under the tongue of the envelope and pried it out with a crinkling sound of dry paper, I think for a second, I sort of had a little fantasy of seeing an address inside and delivering them all those years late.

There wasn't any address.

There wasn't any date, either — and that surprised me, because it was old paper, nice paper, that had been written on with a fancy ink pen or something, and I thought of all my lessons letter writing at school, and how you always had to put the address and the date in the top right corner, and put your address to, and all that.

Dear Peter, the letter started, and it made a shudder run down my spine because I remembered that horrible whispered voice right in my ear at the chapel again, and I put the letter down and went to turn my sausages over, and kind of stood there staring blankly out into the dark of the yard before I steeled myself and went back to it.

* * *

Dear Peter,

I miss you.

I know you'd laugh to hear it from me, and it is stupid, I know it is, but I keep thinking of the bit in my novels where the heroine thinks the hero has gone off for ever, when she thinks he's dead or that he's gone away to war forever, and then he hoves in out of the darkness to embrace her, and she's so happy she could die.

I keep hoping that will happen, that you'll come home, and I understand why you won't, but I still miss you.

I always thought of heartache as something metaphorical, a literary trope invented purely for the purposes of fiction, and yet when I think of you now, I know that I was always wrong: my heart does ache, Peter. It's a sort of dull, hollow pain in the very core of my chest, a painful emptiness, like a part of me is missing — and I suppose a part of me is, because I thought when first we met that we were part of one another.

I think of you near constantly. There hasn't been a moment of the day since you left me that I haven't thought of you.

I think of the way you always used to pick up the music box off the shelf in the antique shop and wind it up, and how you'd dance around as I sat behind the desk with my hand on my chin and watched you, and laughed, because you were ridiculous — and do you remember, Peter, you'd say, "You must never sell this, you know, or I'll simply cease to come back."

And I said, "I don't see why I should care if you come back or not — you never buy anything."

"Maybe I'm sizing something up," you'd say, with that wry grin of yours, and I'd feel exhilarated and my cheeks would burn, and I'd have to duck into the back office to do something to cope — or my mother or father would call me from the workshop, and interrupt.

I play memories of you, Peter, the way you used to wind up that music box — I wind them up and dance with them, at all hours of the day.

I think of the first time you stood next to me in church, and you stood so close to me, and I didn't have the slightest idea what you were at, and when your hand brushed mine I thought that it was an accident even though it made the back of my neck burn, because when I looked at you your gaze was focused forward, listening intently to the sermon — but you were smiling, and I hoped, I hoped so desperately, that it was for me, and when it turned out that it was, I thought I'd drop dead of it.

I never used to tell you you were handsome, did I?

I always thought it, you know.

I didn't want to tell you because I knew that you already knew, and if I said it it would only go to your head, but I always thought you were handsome, always thought you were impossibly charming. I know you loved to make fun of my books, Peter, but when you mocked up the heroes in the books I read, when you brushed your hands through your beard or when you pretended to fence with an invisible sword, or just when you pulled your shirt open and showed your chest hair and asked if I wanted to stroke it until I all but cried with laughter, you really did resemble one of them.

When I walk past the chapel, now, I look up at the bell tower and I think of all the times we used to spend together in there — how I'd sit there by candlelight with my book, and I always meant to keep an eye out for you, but as I waited, I'd get so into the story that I'd be enveloped in it, and I wouldn't hear you come in.

I wouldn't know you were there at all, but then you'd blow out the candle, and as shocked as I'd be by the darkness, as breathless I would be with surprise, I'd feel like a balloon about to burst because I'd feel so much joy, because you were there and we were alone together, and I used to dream about the way you laughed into my mouth when you bent to kiss me.

Do you remember, Peter, how after you lit the candle again, hours later, you'd always grab whatever romance I'd been reading, and you'd quickly rush to read the last page? It used to infuriate me that you'd do that, but now I think of it it makes my heartache worse.

I remember you said to me once, "I have to know how it ends!"

"But you're not even reading the rest!"

"That doesn't matter," you said. "We're all just endings, really — it's the ending that makes a romance, beloved. All that comes before doesn't matter."

And you dropped the book in your lap and cupped my hands in yours and you bent and kissed the backs of my knuckles and it was so impossibly romantic, the two of us lit by candlelight, I almost imagined that in a hundred years, we might be able to be on a cover of a book like that ourselves.

I didn't know it would end the way it did, and I don't suppose you did either.

Oh, Peter.

I miss you. I miss you, I miss you, I miss you — I could write those three words forever like I was writing punishment lines back in the schoolhouse, but they wouldn't do anything, would they?

I find myself talking to you, sometimes, as if you're there, when I'm alone in the shop. What with Mum and Dad and now you too, it seems like everybody in the world has abandoned me at once, and I know that's a terribly selfish way of looking at it, but I just feel so dreadfully alone, Peter.

Maybe it's because they've been gone for longer, but I don't find myself talking to my parents, just to you — I have dreams, sometimes, that you answer me back from wherever you are, and they feel so very real.

I thought a letter would help.

I think it has, even if only in a small way.

I miss you, Peter — I love you still. I hope you know that.

Your beloved

* * *

It was an impossibly intimate letter that I was holding in my hand, I realised, and once I'd finished it, I hurriedly folded it away and put it back in the envelope like I was frightened of someone catching me. It really did feel shameful, you know, looking over someone's shoulder at the aftermath of their break-up, and I felt like it was very wrong of me to have looked — and at the same time, I wanted to read the next one, and I felt very bad about that, too.

I didn't read the next one right away.

Perhaps if I had, what happened next wouldn't have happened — I'm really not sure.

But what I did after reading the first was I put the letter back in the stack with the letters, and I opened the drawer at the bottom of the kitchen drawers and slid it in on top of the fire blanket, and I focused on making my breakfast.

That's the last thing I remember about that day — my hip gave a little bit of a twinge, and I shifted my weight onto my good leg, and I remember turning to the fridge and getting the bacon out, and the carton of eggs, too. I remember, a bit more fuzzily, then, cracking open one of the eggs.

After that...

All the lights went out.

And I mean all of them, not just the lights in the house, not just the light bulbs, but the little red light that showed that the hob was turned on and the green lit-up numbers that showed on the microwave and what little sun had just been starting to show wanly through the clouds outside, that was snuffed out too.

It was so, so dark, and I was so frightened, and I remember trying to cry out, but my mouth wouldn't move, and I was so very cold I really, genuinely, thought that I was dying. It was a cold like I'd never felt in my life, even after the year I swam in the sea on new year's day a few years before to help raise money for a cancer charity, and I came out with my teeth chattering and my body shaking, feeling like I'd never be warm again.

This cold wasn't like that.

When I was cold from that, from the damp, there was a sort of strange feeling to it — my body was very cold, my skin, that is, but I could feel how hot the inside of my chest was, and as numb as my hands and feet were, my blood felt so hot in my gut that I felt like it would *burn* me, the difference between the temperatures I was at on the inside and the outside were so different.

This cold wasn't like that at all.

There was no hot burn in the centre of my chest — there was just more cold, and it was so all-encompassing, so oppressive, so painful, I couldn't breathe, couldn't shout for help, couldn't even *think*, really. I felt a vague terror but I couldn't even concentrate on that because the freezing cold was needling at me, and I didn't think it was ever going to stop, it felt *eternal*.

I couldn't move an inch, ramrod straight with my back lent back against one of the kitchen counters, and when I felt a tear run down my cheek, it felt so cold I thought it must have turned to ice before it reached my beard.

I couldn't tell you how long it lasted.

I was fucking insensate to whatever time even meant anymore, I was sat there for however long, and then there was a sudden burst of extremely bright light — but for how bright it was, it was still very very cold, like when the sun shines very brightly on a snowy day, and the reflection off the snow hurts your eyes.

But there was this painful flash of light, and I saw a man crouched in front of me, and he wasn't like the skinny man I'd seen before — this man, even crouched down, was built more like me: he was broad and heavy. Because the bright light was behind him, I couldn't really make out his face except for his eyes, which were a sort of flinty grey colour, and the curve of his smile shadowed horribly on his face — I knew that he was handsome, but in that light, with those horrible shadows, it was twisted, somehow.

And then the light went out again, and I was in the dark, and the coldness was fading quickly like I'd been dropped into a very hot bath, and it really did burn, it hurt. I sort of hissed and fidgeted on the floor and tried to shake out my frozen joints, and I became aware that my bacon was burned to a crisp and the smoke detector was screaming, and Wodehouse was frantically walking back and forth over my legs and trying to put his paws on my chest and miaowing at the top of his lungs.

The bottom drawer was open.

The lockbox was open too.

The letter I'd already read, I realised when I, with trembling hands, picked up the letters again, had been moved to the back of the pile, so that it was easier for me to read the next one.

Like a ghost's fucking answer to the modern man's Netflix queue.

* * *

I took up the box, putting it aside, and I gave up with breakfast, tossing the burnt to a crisp sausage and bacon aside, because they were so close to charcoal even Wodehouse wasn't interested in them, and my eggs had all but evaporated.

I walked out of the house with the lockbox with me, and went to the chapel — it was past seven, but I did get there earlier than I ordinarily would have, and when I went in, I went straight into the office, putting the letters on my desk and lighting a fire.

I think that was why I wanted to be in the chapel, maybe — it could have been something else, but I wanted to be next to a nice fireplace, wanted to feel its heat. The cold had faded away, but I remembered it keenly — I still remember it now, more vividly than I'd want.

I was slow walking to work, and I was slow sitting down in the chair beside the fire, too — the cold was a memory, but my bad hip felt stiffer and sorer than ever, and I sat there for a few moments and rubbed at it, as if that'd make a difference.

Then, I reached for the next one.

* * *

Dear Peter,

I've been thinking of you this week.

You know that, of course, you have to know it, even if you never read this letter, never know of its contents, but I've been thinking of you constantly, always, always, I think of you. In my dreams, we're together in the chapel belltower, laid out on the picnic blanket you stole from your sister the first time we crept up there together, and you showed me the wood-floored room above the hanging bell, and said, "This shall be our sanctum, beloved: look, let me christen it!" and you spread the blanket out on the floor.

How many hours in our lives, in the decade we've had together — if we can call it being together — do you think the two of us have spent laid on that blanket together, our legs entangled, a romance novel abandoned on the corner of the blanket beside us?

I remember, I used to find it so very cold in the tower, when I was ringing the bell with the others, but somehow, when it was the two of us, it never bothered me. Sometimes, my wrist would twinge if it was very cold — do you remember that? — and you'd notice my little wince, and you'd pick up my hand so gently and lay kisses along the skin, and say you were pouring love into the wound.

I've been thinking of that a lot.

But...

But, Peter.

I know I talk out loud sometimes, and I know I miss you, but I'm so certain that you're listening at my door sometimes, even though you don't answer me, and it drives me so crazy. You mustn't do that, Peter.

I do miss you, and I do want you, and I do love you, but, Peter, you mustn't do that.

It frightens me.

It frightens me so badly — didn't you hear me last night, when I asked you to stop, and to go away?

But I knew that you were there. I couldn't hear you, exactly, and of course I couldn't see you, but I was so very certain that you were just there on the other side of the door, and even though I started talking more, even though I was talking to you, until I was begging, Peter, you can't just—

You can't do that, you mustn't.

You mustn't listen like that, and never say anything — but you mustn't say anything either. You must stop this, Peter.

It isn't right.

And it does pain me to write this, because I love you, and I miss you so very badly, and though a part of me swells to feel you there, you are gone from me for a reason, and you mustn't frighten me like that.

If you loved me, Peter, you wouldn't scare me so.

Your beloved

* * *

I don't think I even breathed between reading that one and picking up the next one. I folded it up and put it back into its envelope, and I picked up the next one, I think, before I'd even considered what I was doing. I did it on autopilot, almost, or automatically.

* * *

Dear Peter,

You woke me last night, Peter.

It doesn't make it better for you to come to me when I'm not awake.

It's been difficult for me to sleep, these past few days — I've been trying so hard not to speak out loud, thinking of you, trying not to talk to you again, because I think I almost convinced myself I had just gone a little mad, that I'd had a little episode and upset myself, that that was all it was. I've had such a stressful year, after all, and that sort of thing happens to a man from time to time, and I believed...

What made you do it, Peter?

Did I say your name when I was sleeping?

You used to tell me I talked in my sleep, and the first time you told me that, after I'd fallen asleep with my head in your lap in the belltower on a warm summer's evening, where we'd snuck up although it was still so light outside, I had such a vivid imagining of the two of us sharing a bed, some time in the future, if we could ever go away from here and have a sort of marriage for ourselves, no matter what our families would think, what anyone would say.

It seemed so wholly and entirely darling, the very thought of the two of us laid in the same bed together, side by side, our hands entwined while we slept, although you said you'd never be able to sleep a wink lying at my side, because I talked even more sleeping than I did awake.

I remember when you told me that it took me by surprise, and I was worried you really hated that part of me, that you were speaking candidly when you said you would never share a bed with me, and oh, Peter, if you could only have seen your own face, the way it crumpled, your mouth falling open, your brows furrowing.

You cupped my cheeks and held me so close to you, and said, "Beloved, beloved, I would sleep beside you 'til the end of time if someone offered it to me, no matter how much you babbled."

Was that it, Peter?

Did I say your name?

It gave me such a shock, that knocking at the door, and I'm sorry to say this and I hope it doesn't wound you but in that moment, I forgot about you, Peter, for the first time in all these months I forgot about you, and sleepily and confusedly I tumbled from my bed and I rushed to the door to see who was knocking so loudly and I pulled the chain out of the loop and I opened the door and I stared out into the empty corridor, into the deep, heavy blackness of it, and all at once, Peter, I remembered.

Did you listen to me cry?

That was wrong of you, Peter.

You mustn't ever do it again. It hurts me so much, to know that you might be so close to me, but that you would then hide from me — I already feel mad with grief, and you needn't compound it.

I'm sorry I forgot you. Even for a moment, to have forgotten you, it feels like the most awful of crimes, but it was only a moment, and even having forgotten you for but a second, I still loved you so dearly: love of you, Peter, is my natural state, and it will be my natural state until the day I die.

But you mustn't hurt me like this.

Not again.

Your beloved

* * *

Horrible, creeping shudders went through me as I sat beside the fire with that letter in my hand, and I think I sat there for quite a while, waiting for the shivers to pass, but whenever I thought they were almost done with, they'd start up again.

It was a sort of fucking...

I don't know.

It was creepy is what it was. It scared me.

I had to open up the graveyard, though, so I put the letters in their lockbox, and I put them into my top drawer in the desk, and I locked the desk drawer to keep what had happened earlier from happening again, and then I picked up my keys and I walked out in the yard.

Before I stepped past the chapel wall, I braced myself, expecting to see the silhouette I'd seen the night previous standing on the path again, but I didn't, and I thanked my lucky stars as I went to open the side gates.

An older woman who worked in the corner shop met me as I went to unlock the other gate, and she had a few questions about how she'd go about getting a grave plot, and she had other questions about the cemetery too — she wanted to know where the oldest graves were, and she was interested in the chapel itself, and even though I didn't know too much, I did my best to answer where I could.

She used to take grave rubbings, she said, when she was a little girl.

I never even learned that woman's name, and never spoke to her again — I don't know if she's dead by now, because she was only sixty or so when I met her, but I think she realised, one way or another, that I was shaken, and I think she talked to me for longer than she'd meant to, and although she glanced down at my cane once or twice, and rushed to hold the door to the chapel open for me like I'd collapse into dust if I tried to pull it open myself, she didn't say a word about it, and didn't stare or make any funny remarks.

I was very grateful, at the time.

It didn't make me forget what I'd been reading, what had been happening to me, but it let me think about something else for a little while, and after she left, I went back to scrubbing the pews, and had them finished up.

I worked through forms after I broke for my lunch, and then, I picked up another letter. It was a little past five o'clock, and already beginning to go dark.

I'm sorry, my hands are shaking a bit badly as I write this now — it's not from remembering, I think, it's rereading the letters, transcribing them.

I forgot how it felt to read them — they feel so real to me. Maybe it doesn't come across on your screen, because it doesn't on mine — maybe it's holding the paper in my hand, smelling the tin and the old paper, or maybe it's just that he wrote those letters, that he held them, that...

Well.

I can't transcribe another just now.

I'll write again soon.

Part 3

Alright.

I've a cup of tea in front of me, I have Wodehouse purring on his little cushion on my desk, and behind me in the kitchen, Gez is laughing at some show on the radio as he does the washing up.

It helps, having him there, it really does — he's not even looking at me, but just the fact that he's there is, Christ, I don't know, something sentimental. Medicine for the soul.

Next letter.

***

Dear Peter,

We've talked about this, Peter.

I can hear you moving about downstairs when the shop is closed for the evening, can hear your footsteps creaking on the boards, hear the soft clink of the teacups when you touch them in their display case, hear the rattle and ring of the register as you open it and close it again.

I wish you wouldn't, Peter.

I won't give into it, you know, I won't rush down to see if you're there — it's such a ghastly thing to do, Peter, don't you know that? Don't you know how ghastly this all is?

It's so very dreadful, you know, because I think of all the times that you wished you were invisible, so that you could creep into the shop and past my parents at all hours of the day and come up to my room without them knowing, and all the times I wished that we could both be invisible, that we might walk hand-in-hand up the street together, or sit on a park bench, or go to dinner, and not worry.

How naïve I was, to want such things as that.

I'd never let a single person see my face again if it meant that I could have you back, Peter, and have you back properly — but that's not what this is, and I know it, and, Peter, you know it too.

You'll make me quite insane.

And people in the village already look at me like I'm quite tragic — it's to do with my parents, of course, not to do with you, but it still makes me so sore, the way people pretend not to stare when I go into the grocer's or dip into church, and sometimes, young people will come into the shop ostensibly to look at the books, and I don't mean to be cruel to them, and not one of them has ever so much as jostled something in passing, let alone broken it, but the boys do stare at me, and I wish they wouldn't.

Sometimes I don't open the shop for days on end, and I just lie in my bed with books, but as much as I look at the text and I turn the pages, I take so little of it in.

It feels as though I've not enjoyed a romance since you left me, Peter, not even the most torrid of them.

What is the point of it, if I'll never know real romance again?

This isn't a romance, anymore, Peter, and you know I never cared for ghost stories.

Please, Peter, I can't stand it.

You mustn't come again.

Your beloved.

* * *

Dear Peter,

I was weak last night, answering the phone, and I wished I hadn't done it as soon as my hand closed around the receiver, but it was as though my arm were moving without my permission, the action already half begun, that I couldn't stop my hand in its tracks as I lifted it up to my ear.

I don't think you know how mad you've driven me this past week, ringing so incessantly as you have, ringing the shop phone and the one upstairs, at all hours of the day.

It's so horrible, Peter.

Whenever I've picked up the shop phone this week and heard silence on the other end of the line, it's stunned me, punched through me like something aiming for my heart, and I've no doubt you've seen how it affects me.

I'm losing weight, Peter. I'm pale and I'm thinner than I used to be and I'm still losing weight — I can scarcely eat, and my eyes are horribly shadowed from lack of sleep, and I can't so much as pick up a pen without trembling. Don't you care about that? Won't you stop until I look as dead as you do?

Even when I fall asleep for a little while, the dreams of you are so terrible — I dream of you alive and big and handsome and holding me, and the joy of it is so strong it is agonising in my sleep, and when I wake and it all goes away again, it hurts more badly than anything has ever hurt me before.

But for losing you the first time, that is.

Was it a kindness, calling all night, and stopping me from sleeping at all?

I couldn't stand it, Peter. I really couldn't stand it — there were tears in my eyes when I finally went to the phone in the hall and I thought I'd rip the unit off the wall, and my knees went weak as I fell against the hall table and held the phone in the crook of my shoulder and gripped at the phone wire, and I listened to the silence on the other end of the phone.

Could you hear me breathing, Peter?

I couldn't hear you.

That's the real cruelty of all this.

You make me feel like I'm going mad. I know that you're there, but when I go to look, or listen, when I reply to you, and there is no sign that you're there except that I know you're there, it's...

When does it stop, Peter?

When does it end?

Did you watch me as I sank down to the floor with the phone in my hand, and crawled to the front door, so that I could listen to the silence on the phone with one ear and know that you were on the other side of the door with the other, so that I knew you were there, and all around me, and still not there at all?

When I slept, I dreamt you were holding me.

I could have died right there.

Your beloved

* * *

As I finished that letter, there was laughter again in the chapel, and this time, I really could hear where it was coming from, could hear its soft echo from the belltower — it was louder than it should have been, because I don't think, when the stairs were still there, that I'd've been able to hear it from down here.

It did sort of narrow down the window that the two lovers, Peter and his girlfriend, must have been alive for — they must have been alive before the stairs had crumbled in the belltower, so the letters were at least fifty years old, and that did make sense to me, what with the whole thing of secrecy.

I'm sure you've realised by now that Peter's beloved was a man, but I didn't even consider that at the time — stupid, I know, but I guess it just didn't click in my head, forty years old, had never really been on a date with someone. It was the early noughties, you know, gays were making strides and all that, but for me, I still didn't really think of us as being romantic — or if we were, I wasn't part of it, and I wasn't a fun, slutty gay either, I was just a guy with a cat and a limp, and there was nothing fun about that.

Maybe if this had all happened to me now, having met Gez, having been with him for so long — married and everything, which as you can imagine, my mother was thrilled about — I might have realised right away.

Or, maybe I wouldn't have.

Gay or not, I'm kind of a stupid guy.

The laughter spooked me a little, and I folded the letter I'd just read and put it away, and I walked outside to lock up the side gates. It was getting darker and darker as I limped up the path, my lantern in the other hand. My hip was sorer than usual, that day — even though the horrible cold from that morning had faded away, I could still feel the stiffness it had left behind, and the bone on that side felt heavier than on the other.

The silhouette of the man on the path didn't surprise me, this time — no, that's a lie, it did scare me, but I also expected it to be there. I didn't stop walking, didn't stop even for a moment: I just kept walking forward, and this time, it faded in front of my eyes, like how smoke dissipates.

I stood where the ghost had stood, and I faced the way he'd been facing, and I looked down at the grave closest to the path.

PETER DENBOROUGH, it said, **LOVING BROTHER.**

The dates were underneath: 26th May 1931–26th December 1959.

I don't know how long I stood there for, staring down at that gravestone. A lot of the graves that were that old were a little messy and overgrown, but this one was well taken care of, I could tell. There was a bouquet of fresh flowers resting on the grass of the grave bed, and there was no moss or anything growing on the stone — it looked very clean.

I remember that struck me, somehow.

This'll make me sound like a prick, but at the time I thought, God, imagine having someone love you enough to think you're haunting them, and have someone else take care of your grave, to have two people who loved you like that. I knew that they were different, and that Peter's beloved was dead.

I stood there for a long time, staring down at the headstone, and then I limped along and locked the other gate, but when I came back to the chapel, the lights were on inside again, and it scared me shitless until I crossed over the threshold and saw Arthur standing there.

"Pastor," I said, and he turned to look at me, smiled. He was wearing his coat still, although it really wasn't that cold inside, and the old man smiled at me as I came back inside.

"You really look a bit creepy with that lantern like that, you know, like a spectre," he said quietly. "Your granddad used to use it for Halloween."

"I didn't know that," I said, putting it gently down on one of the pews."

"You have the place looking well," he murmured, gesturing to the room.

I'd managed to dust most of the cobwebs out of the eaves and off the beams with a mop on a long pole, as much as it had been a balancing act, and I'd done the same thing with the windows, cleaning off the marks and dust from the stained glass frescos; the pews were clean and I'd put a coat of wood polish on them, and beaten out the rug that ran up toward the stage so that it had gone back to being red instead of grey.

"There's still a lot to do," I said. "Are you here for anything in particular?"

"Oh, I saw the light, that's all," the pastor said, giving a wave of his hand. "I thought it was…" He trailed off, shook his head, and chuckled. "Well. I realised it was your lantern. You were out there for longer than usual."

"I was looking at one of the graves," I said. "Peter Denborough, did you know him?"

"Of course," the old man said. "He died a few years before you were born, of course, you'd never have met him, and his sister doesn't live in the village anymore, she just comes every few months to visit his grave. What made you look at him?"

"He died on Boxing Day," I said, because it was true, and I had thought about it, and I thought it might make me sound a little less bonkers than if I said that I thought he'd been haunting me.

"Terrible thing," Arthur said quietly, nodding his head in a slow, sage way. "It was a car accident — he was a solicitor, and he worked in... Oh, I don't know, I don't really remember anymore — in town, anyway, and he was driving back to the village. It was too wet for the snow to settle, but there was slush and ice on the roads. It was a horrible wreck. He was a bit like you, actually — a very nice young man, but..." He stumbled over his words for a second, before he settled on, "Unmarried."

And then he smiled in a fragile, hurried way, like he was scared of hurting my feelings, but luckily for him, I was a fucking idiot, and didn't understand what he was insinuating about me — or Peter Denborough — until I was home in bed that night.

I didn't ask him about the letters just yet. It didn't feel like the right time to.

I thought about Peter Denborough and his sister who loved him and the car accident he was in and his well-maintained gravestone and his beloved, and it wasn't until after I was laid down in my bed, trying to convince Wodehouse that he shouldn't put the whole of his weight directly on my throat, that I realised what the pastor said, and realised at the same time that I'd forgotten the letters at the church, and then the horrible, dead cold feeling set in again, and I couldn't even struggle, and I laid like that all night, because I couldn't break loose of it until the sun came up.

I cried when it let me free.

They weren't tears of relief or anything like that — I cried so hard with terror and nausea and pained fear of the unknown that it *hurt*, that I felt like every tear squeezed out of me would bruise my cheeks, and I was late to work by a few hours.

Not that anyone noticed.

Not anyone alive, anyway.

* * *

Dear Peter,

It reminded me, last night, of the first time you taught me to dance.

You'd snuck into the shop by the back window when my mother and father were up in London — how I wish we could have had more moments like that together — and came up to my bedroom, and you put the needle delicately down against the vinyl, and you chalked out your steps on the ground so that I could follow them and do as you did.

It felt like that, last night.

Like you were stepping into the chalk marks I left on the floor, like you were shadowing me — like you were my ghost, instead of your own.

I could feel you there as I walked to and fro in the flat, and I knew that you were there, a hair's breadth from me, and I was so certain if I simply turned my head I would see you out of the corner of my eye and know you to be there, but whenever I looked, I didn't see you.

I don't know if it is getting easier.

Will you be with me like this, always?

I don't think I could bear it, Peter. You must go — you should go. This isn't right.

Do you haunt Christine like this?

I couldn't sleep last night, knowing you were there, standing over me, watching me, and I wanted more than anything for you to crawl into bed with me and wrap your arms around me and hold me and you didn't, Peter, you just stood there and looked down at me, the way I stand over your grave sometimes when I know that Christine will be at work and won't come by.

Mr Darvill is so kind to me, you know, the way he always was, but kinder than usual, and it seems to me that now you're gone, he's the only man in the world that knows who I am, and he barely knows anything about me at all.

I think he takes these letters when I leave them on your grave, Peter.

They're never there when I walk by twice in a day.

That's very good of him, I think. He always greets me by name when he sees me, and asks me in that sort of soft, quiet way that some people do how I am, but he's the only one that knows that when I come into the cemetery every day, it isn't my parents' grave I linger by.

I miss you, Peter.

I miss you more and more, the more that you are with me. Even as I write this, I feel you hovering behind me, reading over my shoulder — Peter, I am so, so alone, and it's only worse knowing you're with me.

When you finally do go, I don't know how I'll cope.

Your beloved

* * *

Gez has run a bath for us, and if the idea of two old men crammed into a bath together sounds stupid and uncomfortable and ridiculous, you'd be right, but they're also surprisingly nice, and he always plays some stupid television show on his iPad when we do it, and we drink a glass of wine together, and the hot soak of the water is good for my hip.

Hope you don't take it personally, but a hot bath with my husband's a bit more appealing right now than writing all this horrible stuff down to be read — and I know I started writing it and I know I have to write it down, or the dreams won't ever stop again, but it's hard.

It's tough.

More soon.

Part 4

Dear Peter,

Sometimes when I read my books these days, I think about the way you would read to me — I think about the countless times we lay together in the belltower, the only warmth to be found in each other, my cheek rested on your chest, as you read aloud from whatever book I was reading and mocked every line in the same breath, but you always did it with such affection.

It never wounded me.

Sometimes, the way people talk about books like that, they do it with such scorn — they are disgusted by the delight with which so many people read them, criticise the women (and they only ever mention women) who read them, say that they are lacking in character or plot or craft, and it is so derisive that it does wound.

Not when you made fun of them, Peter.

It made me laugh, when you made fun.

You always sounded as affectionate about the books as I did.

Last night, as I locked the door to the shop, it took me by surprise when the music box began to chime its tune, and it shocked me so much it hardly even occurred to me to cry. I just stood there, stock-still, watched the little dancer spin in front of the mirror, listened to the song.

I can never remember what it's called. Mozart or Beethoven or one of them, I know you told me, Peter, I know you told me a dozen times, but I don't remember anymore what it was, and I hardly have anyone left I can ask.

Last night, when you sat on the bed beside me, I felt the mattress depress, and I didn't dare open my eyes because I didn't want you to rush away if I tried to look at you, and I wanted so badly to feel you warm on the bed beside me, and you weren't cold, even — just there. I fell asleep imagining you were stroking my cheek, and woke again when you knocked on the walls so hard that dust fell from the rafters.

I miss you, Peter.
Your beloved

*　* *　* *　*

Dear Peter,

I saw Christine yesterday.

I didn't know that she'd recognise me, not from the one time that she caught a glimpse of me climbing out of your bedroom window — perhaps she didn't recognise me at all, but simply knew that there had been a man, that you'd had one.

I didn't see her before she saw me. I was lost in my own world, standing over your grave and huddled in my coat, speaking under my breath to you, and she must have had a moment to rev up her engines, so to speak, because when she ran up to me it was with more fury than I've ever seen.

"Get the fuck away from him!" she screamed at me, like the harpy she always was. "You have no right, no right, get away from here!"

That wasn't all she said, of course. She had a lot of other choice words besides, but they were the sort of words you never liked to hear — the sort of words you used to tell me you'd rinse out of my mouth, if you ever heard me repeating them.

It used to make me smile, when you said things like that.

I don't really smile at anything anymore.

I know she's your sister, Peter — I know you loved her, that you were always patient with her, but as much as she loved you, she hated what you were, what we were. But I don't know how you used to stand it, the way that she was — I don't know how you stand it now.

Perhaps that's why you haunt me instead of her.

I hate to ache for you, Peter, the way that I do, desperate for you to touch me again and knowing that you won't.

When you knocked on the door last night I ran so fast that I tripped on the rug, but I thought in the moment that if I couldn't only get there fast enough, haul the door open fast enough, pull the phone off the receiver fast enough, answer you fast enough, that you might really, truly be there.

But you weren't, Peter.

The hallway was as empty as always; the phone was as silent as always; I was alone as always.

It isn't fair.

Your beloved

* * *

After work that day, I walked over to the church proper, and caught the end of the church choir's rehearsal, watched all of them singing — they were readying Christmas carols leading up to the season, and it sounded good to me, not that I knew anything about music at the time, or even know anything about it now.

Arthur was stood at the front, but he wasn't the conductor — the conductor was a tiny old woman who had taught me maths at school, and as tiny as she was, she had lungs on her like a fucking bellows, could produce sound you'd never expect from someone her size.

When Arthur saw me, he looked at me with concern, raised his eyebrows as if to ask if I needed him right this second, but I shook my head, mouthed it was okay, and waited for them all to finish.

I heard someone call her Christine, and I turned to look at a tall, thin woman in a burgundy jumper, wearing pearls. She looked very neat and well put-together, but there was a gauntness in her cheeks like she didn't get enough to eat.

"I'm going to go along to Peter now," I heard her say to one of the other women, and I watched her friend step back to let her pass, watched her pick up a little box of flowers to put on his grave.

It had begun to drizzle outside, but that didn't seem to deter her, and I said, "The side gates are locked, Miss. You'll have to use the main gate."

She sniffed at me, looking at me with a haughty look on her face, glancing down at my cane. "You're Raymond Darvill's boy. His grandson. I don't see how anyone can dig graves with a cane."

"Er, I don't," I said. "I've been cleaning up the chapel, and I keep the books in order. I used to be a postman."

Something changed in her face, a sort of catch, and I watched her lips downturn slightly, saw the expression of something almost like sympathy as she glanced down at my cane again.

"Car accident," I said.

She nodded, stoutly, and then she walked off very hurriedly, the block heels of her boots making a loud click-clack on the stone floors.

"She was very gentle with you," said Arthur, and I huffed out a low, almost-laugh as I followed the old man toward his office, standing with my back toward the old halogen heater so I could let it warm my backside and my sore hip — the rain was tugging at it, it seemed to me, and making it worse than usual, that day.

"I wanted to, I wanted to ask you a question," I said haltingly, tapping my fingers against the side of the cane's handle, pressing against the varnished wood every few moments.

"Ask away," Arthur said, sinking slowly down into his chair with a soft sigh.

"My granddad," I said. "If he saw letters on a grave, what would he do with them?"

"Leave them," the pastor said, looking at me funny, his thick, furry eyebrows furrowing together, like two kissing caterpillars. "He left everything on a grave as long as he could without it causing a problem."

I looked at him. I don't know what my face looked like, don't know if it showed on my face what I wanted, what I expected him to say next, but I watched him sort of falter, his lips parting, and he looked at my all serious, concentrated, and then he slowly crossed his arms loosely over his chest, leaning back in his chair so that it gave a musical creak.

"This is about Peter Denborough," he said slowly.

"Yeah," I said. When he said nothing, I said, "You knew — You knew, right? About his boyfriend? He wrote letters. It looks like my granddad picked them up. To keep Christine from... You know."

"Yeah," Arthur said. "Yes. She's not as volatile as she used to be."

"Still a homophobe?"

"Don't look at me," Arthur said. "It's not what I preach."

I laughed, dragging my thumb over my lip, and then I asked, "Did you know about his boyfriend? At the time? Before he died?"

"Yes, I knew," Arthur said. "I never knew who he was, but I knew that Peter had a regular... Boyfriend, if that's what you want to call it. Christine mentioned it to me a few times, she wanted it to stop — it was still illegal then, you understand. A lot of police would be very glad to... Well. It wasn't talked about, and I think Christine had an understanding that she was well off enough that she could ensure Peter got away with everything his partner didn't. She wanted to know what his name was, always asked me if I knew."

"But you never did?"

"No," Arthur said quietly.

"His parents were dead," I said. "They both died, I think maybe the same year Peter did, and I think he ran an antique shop, but there's no shop like that I know of in the village today. Does any of that ring a bell?"

It was a subtle change in the pastor's face. His eyebrows jumped up a tiny bit, his lips went sort of loose on his face, and I saw his eyes move a little, like he was studying something I couldn't see — realising something I wouldn't know anything about.

"No," he said. "No, it doesn't."

I knew it was a lie, and I think that in that moment, he knew that I knew I was lying, but the two of us just stood there, looking at each other, and then I nodded again, wrapping my hand more solidly around the handle of my cane.

There was one final letter for me waiting at the chapel, and I was terrified to face another night as a corpse, so I didn't go home, but walked back to the chapel and stepped inside. Christine was already gone by the time I went back to the graveyard, but I didn't mind that.

I wouldn't have to talk to her until later.

* * *

Dear Peter,

I can't stand it, Peter.

I'll die.

I'll die if you keep doing this to me, and I'll die so slowly, Peter, so torturously, of sleep deprivation or starvation or just of heartache, and I can't bear it, I can't bear it anymore, because I want you back so badly, I need you, and I feel like you're just behind a shroud, just out of my grasp.

Do you remember, Peter, how we used to meet?

How I'd light a candle and sit with my book and when you came into the bell tower you'd blow out the candle, and in the dark, we'd be together again?

I know I mustn't ask, Peter.

I know I mustn't encourage it.

I know I told you you shouldn't and that I didn't want you to do this and I know I told you that you had to leave, but, Peter...

Tonight, Peter.

Tonight, I will light a candle in the bell tower, and I'll wait for you, Peter.

Please, come.

And if you don't, if you don't, then...

Please.

I miss you, Peter. I love you, Peter.

I just need to know what the last page of our book together would have been — I just need to know that I'm not mad, that you're there, really there, I just need a real sign, I need you, Peter.

I'm nothing without you.
I feel sometimes as if I am the ghost you've left behind.
Please come, Peter. Please.
Your beloved

* * *

I don't know how long I stood there in my grandfather's old office, turning the letters over again and again, rifling through their envelopes, looking at the back of the letters, trying to search for any kind of clue or hint as to what it all meant, what came next, but there wasn't anything. Why would there be?

It was a collection of fucking letters from a grieving boyfriend, not a treasure hunt, but...

Well.

I saw through the office window the man standing over Peter's grave, the same silhouette I had seen before, and I rushed to grab my lantern and stumbled as I limped as fast as I could out toward the door, and when I walked out under the rain, my cane and my boots both squelched in the grass.

The silhouette, the ghost, was still there as I walked up the path, until I got close enough, and then it faded away into mist again, like it had before, and I stood there, breathing heavily, feeling the cold, wet air in my lungs, feeling its sting on my cheeks.

Christine's new flowers rested on Peter's grave.

Maybe—

Maybe it had happened before. I would never have seen it from inside of the chapel, but all the times I'd walked the graveyard before, it had been early in the morning or in the evening — it was nearly nine o'clock now.

The candlelight in the belltower flickered slightly, as if someone was moving inside, and it sent a wave of tower running down my spine.

I didn't know, for a second, what the Hell I was supposed to do, didn't understand it, because the stairs had been destroyed, so how was I meant to get up there, *how*...?

And it was like... I don't know, it was light seeing it highlighted, somehow, light there was a spotlight — a car must have passed by, and the light shone on the building exactly where it was supposed to show.

All at once, I saw the low roof of the mausoleum, covered over with turf so that you could walk straight up onto it; I saw the thick, layered ivy up to the flat edge of the end of the chapel roof; I saw more ivy, thick and luscious and green, that led all the way up to the opening of the belltower.

No wonder it was their safe haven, if they started to meet up there after the stairs were gone.

I know it was crazy, and I know I shouldn't have done it, especially not with my hip, but I did — climbing up onto the mausoleum roof was easy, but climbing the ivy up to the first roof and then to the other was probably the most terrifying thing I've ever done in my life. The ivy held as I climbed it, and although I could feel the leaves shift under the weight of my hands and my feet, as I moved up through it, it didn't tear away even slightly from the wall, the ivy was so tightly embedded, so strongly rooted against it.

My hands trembled as I climbed. My hip ached, and the higher I climbed, the keener the pain got. It wasn't really a tall climb at all — like I told you at the start, the actual tower wasn't much taller than a normal house — but I wasn't ever an athlete, and I couldn't even climb trees as a kid, let alone fucking walls.

It hurt.

By fuck, it hurt, hurt more and more and more, and yet somehow, the roaring, screaming pain on the whole of one side of my body as I forced myself to climb higher, shoved myself flat again the building, it drove me onward.

It was agonising, that pain, but it was nothing like the cold, throbbing pain I'd felt in my waking, haunted nightmares — this was a hot, searing pain, and it made me know I was alive.

When I got to the top of the belltower, there was a kind of outer ledge I could get my knees onto, and I rested my hands against the ledge that was a little higher than my head — the edge of the bell tower's room, or entrance, whatever you wanted to call it. I was breathing heavily, and I could taste the torch that I'd decided to carry in my mouth like some idiot cop in an action movie, and it tasted fucking *awful*, like rubber and salt. I hadn't even thought to turn the fucking thing on, so I might as well have left it on the carabiner on my belt.

I hauled myself on shaking, pained legs to look into the bell tower.

The lit candle rested on a little dish, flickering slightly in the wind, and it illuminated the room, which I realised now must have been *over* the bell itself — there was a gap in the centre of the floor where the chain suspended from the frame at the top of the ceiling went through, and I could see the top loop of the bell through the gap.

Beloved's corpse was staring at me from sightless eye sockets. It wasn't a skeleton just yet — the body was shrivelled and rotted and old, but it didn't smell like anything except a sort of musty sweetness, and cobwebs, and dust.

The body had a mildewed old book in its lap, was wrapped in blankets, and I stared at it, stared for—

I don't know how long.

But not long enough that the candle's wick had burned down, and not long enough for a sudden gust of wind.

The candle went out, and the tower was plunged into darkness.

I think I screamed as I fell.

* * *

The most remarkable thing about it, I suppose, is that I didn't have to go to the hospital afterward. I'd had a soft landing somehow, despite the height of the fall, and I had a few bruises on me, but that was all.

When I called the police, they didn't really believe me, and I had to limp into town the next morning to get one of the constables to come along, and Joel, the kid who actually dug the graves, managed to get a cherry picker for us, to bring us up to the bell tower without needing a ladder.

I don't think PC Plod had seen a dead body before, because he vomited over the side of the picker's trough, and there was something artistic about the way the spatter fell all the way down to the grass.

I don't want to tell you his name.

He never signed it, and I feel like it'd be wrong, somehow, to put it out there when he never wanted it put out there, but I'm sure, like anything else, if you really wanted to know it you could probably find it out.

His parents had died, like I'd suspected, in '59, in February of that year, of carbon monoxide poisoning after some sort of leak in their flat, which was above the antique shop in town. When he disappeared, the sad thing was, no one ever noticed. I think he must have gone up there later that February or March, but it wasn't mentioned in the local police reports until July.

It wasn't anything unkind, it wasn't intentional — I don't think so, anyway.

It was just that beloved was telling the truth, when he said Peter was the only connection he'd had left. It seems like people noticed the shop was shut, but everyone just assumed he'd gone off somewhere, and run away. The police report at the time described him as shy, sweet but insular, not comfortable with people.

I tried to tell Christine.

I went up to her, with the letters — the cops refused to take them, what with how they weren't signed or anything, so they didn't count as evidence — I tried to explain, to explain that...

Ah, fuck it.

I don't know what I'd have explained to her, and it doesn't matter either way: she told me to fuck off, and she called me, I'm sure, a lot of the names she'd called beloved.

* * *

For years, I was alright.

I met Gez down in London while on a weekend retreat with my parents, and despite the fact that I told him this from the get-go — almost shamelessly — he fell instantly in love with me, and we've been together ever since.

Disclaimer: that's not exactly, or even at all, how it happened, but the result is the same.

The nightmares started about a year or two after that.

They were intermittent, at first, once or twice a year, and then they happened more often... This year, they've been every week. They weren't the corpse dreams, mostly — I would dream at first that Gez was almost there but I couldn't touch him, couldn't feel him, couldn't see him, but that he was there, just out of my reach, and it was agonising.

But this year, the corpse dreams started happening again.

I knew the whole time I needed to write it down, I knew that I...

They wanted it told, I think, one way or the other.

They wanted those letters read.

I think about it, regularly, I think about it, 'cause it's fucked up.

I love Gez. I love him fiercely, powerfully — I love him in a way I never expected to fucking love anything, anybody, and it's a kind of hot feeling in my chest whenever I look at him, whenever I think of him, and I know he loves me too.

And I read beloved's letters to Peter, sometimes, and I think about the fact that in those letters, there's never any proof he was being haunted at all.

No friends. No family. No one who'd be able to vouch for if he was acting normal or not, if Peter was an actual ghost with him, or if he was just a grieving man gone crazy with grief.

You could say I was crazy, too, and maybe I was, but I do think what I experienced was a haunting, simply because I had to discover things as I went, because I ended up at the end with a corpse — if it was a haunting, I'm uncomfortably prophetic, and I'd rather it was the first thing.

I was haunted. But was beloved?

I don't know.

As I finish this up, I'm watching Gez.

He's fallen asleep on the sofa with Wodehouse collapsed like a ton of chubby bricks on top of him. He's still got his reading glasses on even though he knows it leaves a horrible imprint in the side of his face when he sleeps like that, and his phone is dangling from his hand.

They couldn't find a cause of death for Peter's beloved. The body wasn't well preserved, even though it was put together — it could have been a heart attack, an aneurysm, a heart attack, anything. I wonder sometimes if Peter killed him, or if he just died of grief.

I wouldn't want to do that to Gez — I wouldn't want to haunt him, and I don't think he'd want to haunt me, but if he did, would I go crazy with it? Would I die of it? If I was dead and Gez was still alive, would I torture him so much that he died, just so we could be together?

I hope not.

But I love him, you know. I love him so much, sometimes, I love him so much that I could...

Maybe I won't show him this part.

I feel so... relieved, having written all that down. Like I'm finally free, somehow.

Like it's over.

FIN.

I Forgot My Manners

Manners are very important.

That's my opinion, that's my feeling on the matter — I like to think I'd feel that way even if I didn't come from where I come from, where having good manners is sometimes the difference between life or...

Or an unpleasant alternative.

I don't think I should really say where I come from: if you know the area, I have no doubt you'll recognise it from context clues, and if you don't, that's for the best. It's not that I live in an unpleasant place — on the contrary, as cold and damp as English weather can be from time to time, particularly up here, I live in a beautiful area, and I've always felt very blessed.

Huge swathes of woodland are protected in trust near to where I live, and the village I'm from is a little ways up the mountain, a plateau cut out with paths that lead down through the woodland or further up and along, to join the public thoroughfares, the national walks. There's a lot of wildlife, a lot of deer and birds, wild flowers, and the views are wonderful.

You have to walk sideways and take a few strange turns to make it down to us from the main path. It's very easy for us to make our way out but not so easy for outsiders to make their way in — I would like to tell you it's for their protection, or suchlike, but really it's that outsiders have no manners, and resent the consequences that come of that.

I hope you don't think I have a low opinion of you, presuming you're an outsider, presuming you've never been here — I wouldn't like to make assumptions. Unfortunately, it's always the case that one bad apple spoils the fate of the barrel, and I admit, I'm not myself of late.

I thought writing all this out would help.

It starts with what you'd expect, good manners.

Say please when asking for something, say thank you when it is received. Greet those you meet politely and respectfully. Do not step over boundaries or into spaces where you are not invited. Never take the last morsel from a plate, or the last fruit from a bush. Don't whistle or make a racket when people are trying to sleep.

Help others. Be kind.

Be thoughtful.

Manners are only local customs, you know — there's nothing universal in them, in any of them, whether they're ours or yours. What's important is what the manners communicate — your respect for other people, and for your surroundings.

And here, we have the People.

We call them the People — there are other names for them, but they're too direct, and the People are quite protective of their names and how they're addressed or spoken of. That's about respect, too, not bandying about their proper names without cause, even amongst ourselves, even to outsiders — it would be like gossip, or blasphemy, or something like a mix of both.

The People aren't sacred, you understand — they're not gods, and they're not monsters. They aren't harmful at all, so long as you treat them with respect. I used to be so frightened of them, when I was a child, and I used to cry when they passed us on the woodland paths and hide my face against my mother's waist.

This was rude, but they never made anything of it, even though they would be well within their rights to.

I'm rambling: I'm sorry, it's complicated, and as I said, I'm not myself.

The People are very tall, seven feet at the shoulder, and they walk on two spindly legs with pointed feet, balancing on them — I think they might be hoof-shaped, but they don't make a sound when they move. They have more joints in their long limbs than we do, and far less torso to speak of: their bodies are thickly, densely furred, or at least, their three long fingers on each hand are, and their legs, too. They wear cloaks woven of tree leaves and wildflowers, or pieces of fir in winter, that hide most of their bodies and the backs of their heads, and masks.

The masks are unsettling if you aren't used to them.

I don't know what it is they make them of — they look soft to the touch, like rubber, but I don't know that the People even know what rubber is. They're normally pale pink, and roughly modelled on human features, with eyebrows and painted eyes and carved noses and smiling mouths. The smiles, in the People's masks, are rictus smiles, every dimple and line in the resin expressions exaggerated, the eyes too wide and staring.

They're not meant to be frightening.

The People wear them for our benefit — my mother says they know that they frighten us, even when they don't mean to. They wear their masks to comfort us, so that we see them wear faces like ours.

It's not their fault.

It's what they think we look like — perhaps to the People, we are the ones with exaggerated proportions, with unsettling movements, with frightening appearances.

I don't think so. I don't think the People are frightened of anything.

The People are the reason our manners are so important. Our communication with them is limited. They don't really speak, and I'm not sure they can, because the most I've ever heard of them is breathy, hoarse sounds that I couldn't hope to replicate, and I wouldn't try to.

The People walk in the same woods that we do. They must have settlements, I suppose, although I don't know where they are, and have never come across one, and I couldn't reliably tell two People apart, from one day to the next.

If you're walking in the woods and you come across the People — they never walk alone, only in pairs or more — it is polite to greet them verbally, to smile, and to give a bow of your head. It doesn't have to be a very deep bow — most of us just bow from our shoulders — but a bow is the done thing.

I usually bow first, but that's not a sign of inferiority or anything — sometimes the People bow first, and that's alright, so long as you respond in kind.

Most of the time, that's the end of it — you keep walking one way, and the People keep walking the other way, and perhaps you won't see each other again. They walk in strange ways, the People: their legs are so long and have such odd joints, peeking out from under their swinging cloaks, that it looks sometimes as though they're about to topple, and it's polite to keep a wide berth.

I heard of a boy once who was in a hurry because he had an exam at school and he was running in from his house and he was late, and he skidded to a stop when he saw the People, and he bowed and said hello, and then once they'd bowed back he started running again but instead of keeping to the side of the path he ran straight between the pair of them and knocked one of them over.

That was years ago — my parents went to school with him, and I don't even know his name, only that he stumbled in for his exam three hours late instead of ten minutes and couldn't remember his name, let alone any of the answers.

He was sick, and then he cried, but he didn't cry like a teenager, didn't even cry like a child: my mother said he cried in a desperate, confused way, his voice cracking and choking, making wounded desperate wails, scrambling for someone, something to hold onto, and she said you could tell just from looking at him that he had no idea where he was, no idea who he was, no idea what was happening.

He didn't go back to school after that.

But maybe that's just a story, about him knocking them over — maybe he littered, or took a shortcut he oughtn't have. Perhaps he was rude in some other way.

Perhaps he wasn't rude at all, and the People decided just by looking at him that he deserved it, but I don't like to think about that.

They've never done anything like that before, that I know of, and I don't like to imagine they would.

I want to believe they're kind, the People.

I remember when I was so small, sobbing into my mother's skirt, and the way she tried to be stern with me, tried to tell me, "You have to be polite, say hello, honey, and bow, *please*," and she'd been trying to keep the panic out of her voice, trying not to sound scared, and that just made me cry harder.

One of the People reached out and put its long, inhuman fingers on her shoulder, touched her in a gentle, undemanding way, and breathed out its hard, choking sound, and then the three People had walked on, and left us be.

I greeted the next ones, and it seemed to me that they were more pleased than they ordinarily were, because one of them clapped.

I wonder if they know who I am, me specifically, if they know that I was that same little child, once.

I don't know if that would be good or bad.

It happened the day before yesterday.

I was walking with a friend of mine, Shelley, just a normal, socially-distanced walk through the woods. It was late in the morning on a Saturday, and although we're in the same bubble, because our houses are right next door to one another and Shelley's mother is very close to mine, we were both still wearing our masks. I'd stepped off the path to take a photograph of one of the new daffodils, making sure I wasn't treading over any boundaries or stepping on any other flowers, and Shelley stuck to the edge of it.

She took off her mask to light a cigarette, which I didn't care for, but smoking in itself isn't so bad, and Shelley's always good about carrying the butt with her once she's finished, to toss in a bin, but today she dropped her mask — she wears paper masks still, because she sweats too much, she says, in the cloth ones — and because it had fallen in the mud she kicked it aside to pull another out of her pocket.

"Shelley," I said when I saw her. "Shelley, you can't *do* that."

"Oh, for God's sake," she muttered, "it's filthy, I can't just put it back on, and my hands will be muddy if I pick it up, and it's just a paper mask, what harm—"

"Just wrap it in a tissue or something!"

She looked at me with a scowl on her face, crossed her arms at me all defiantly, as if I were her mum and I was telling her what to do. She's always been like that, sometimes, just hates to be told what to do, would argue with the moon if it told her it was made of moonrock. It annoyed me so much. I was impatient. "I don't have any."

"Well, I do, and it's shitty to just drop it like that, Shell," I muttered, and because I was angry I was in a rush going through my backpack to try to find my tissues, and I dropped my phone, and it slid down the hill.

I ran to get it.

I heard Shelley say hello from where I was rummaging through a patch of wild garlic to find it, and I heard the sharpness in her tone, and I heard the harsh, breathless noise of one of the People. My stomach dropped even as my hand clasped around my phone, and I half-crept up the hill again, trying not to disturb any leaves or sticks or stones, barely even daring to breathe.

From behind a heavy bush I could see the tops of the two People's heads as they stood over Shelley, and from the angle I was at, they were facing away from me, because this was where the path curved.

I could hear how loudly Shelley was breathing.

"Oh, um, no, no, I just dropped it by accident," she was saying, "I obviously wasn't going to leave it here, I just dropped it in the mud, I was only trying to kick it into the water so that it wasn't so — No, no, you don't have to do that, you don't have to do that, please, it's—"

She trailed off and made a sort of sobbing noise, and I realised why because I heard the sort of...

It was a horrible sound.

The masks must have been harder than I thought, because it made a kind of crackling, gory sound as it was peeled off of its face, popping wetly, and I could hear Shelley crying more softly now.

I couldn't see what was underneath, but I saw a glimpse of the mask in its hand as it pulled it away, the thick, congealed purple-redness that dripped away from the back of the humanesque features held in its hand, and I could hear Shelley's breathing quicken even more, hear the sobbing noises she made, the heaving, gagging sounds.

I don't know if the second one took its mask off.

The thing is, the pandemic's actually made it safer, not that it's normally a danger, usually, but...

But the thing is, it's manners, right?

It's manners.

She was sobbing so loudly it cut right through me, and I feel awful for running, but I couldn't bear it, couldn't bear the sound of it ad the idea of the both of them looking at her, but I just ran a ways along the hillside before rejoining the path, and I sprinted into the house and locked the door and didn't go out again.

It's manners.

It's only polite, if one of the People removes their mask, to remove your own.

They found her yesterday. She was still alive, and they got her to the hospital, and I don't know if she's making sense, because from what I heard, she was still gibbering and crying, but I tried to tell her, I did, and she should have known anyway.

They're going to have to do reconstructive surgery, and maybe after that, she'll be alright, I don't know.

I don't know.

My mother isn't home. She's coming back tomorrow, she's just been helping my grandfather for a few days, and I don't want to call her because I'm so bad on the phone, I'll never know how to say it, but I'm so frightened because it was rude, and I know it was rude, and wrong of me.

I should have stopped to explain, I should have picked it up for her and said I was just getting my tissues, I should have tried to help, but I was scared, I was frightened, and it wasn't my fault, none of it, and I didn't want the People to blame me.

What should I do?

Should I do anything? Is there anything I *can* do?

I know you don't know. I don't know either. I don't think anyone knows.

As I finish this post, I can hear our doorbell ringing.

There's no one who'd be coming to visit me, not with Shelley's parents at the hospital, and our deliveries wouldn't come here either. There's no one. There's no one, except...

And a knock, now.

I have to let them in, I've already left it too long.

It's good manners, to greet guests, to invite them in, to offer them food and drink, and I'm so scared I can feel my heart in my throat, but I have to.

I wonder if they'll remember me. I wonder if they'd be merciful twice over, but I'm not a kid anymore, and being scared is no excuse.

I hope they'll be kind.

I hope so.

FIN.

Wild Country

It was one of those spur of the moment decisions that you make when drunk, and you don't realise until you're seeing things in more sober retrospect that... Yeah. Better choices could have been made.

I'd been out at The White Lion for my cousin's birthday party, and the original plan had been to all drive back to hers with her roommate driving. Her roommate had backed out, and luckily for my cousin, her boyfriend had offered to come out and be designated driver. Unluckily for me, they have some of the loudest sex known to man, and there was no way if I went home to hers I'd be able to actually sleep on their sofa — I'd be up for hours listening to them at it.

Anyway, I told them I'd ordered a taxi, which I had done, but after they'd left, I got the confirmation text that it would be a forty-five minute wait. The Lion was still open for another hour or so, but I wasn't in the mood to sit in there on my phone while the music was pounding, and because I was drunk, I just thought, oh, it's not that far of a walk home.

I'll just walk!

It's an hour and a half, if not two, and I live in a village in the valleys, so the main road between the White Lion in this village and home in mine cuts right into the valley side, with a sheer slope on one side down to the river and hewn-back cliff on the other.

I'd say I don't know what I was thinking, but at the end of the day, I wasn't thinking, was I?

I was just drunk and a bit thick, and by the time I'd sobered up enough to think more seriously about things I'd been walking for twenty-five minutes and didn't much feel like turning back.

The winding road is pretty well-lit, but then, it has to be — there's thick forestry on the sloping side, the trees tall and old, and it was blocking out a lot of the light from the moon that night, what little could get through the cloud cover. Still though, with the sharp bends and turns in the road, sometimes, there are places where it's dark at night — the light comes away from the streetlamps and you can actually see the gaps of shadow between the edges of each circle of light, trees making shadows between some of them, or the edge of the cliffs at times. Fog was threatening as I'd started walking in, and once I was beginning to sober up, there was a good deal more of it, enough to add to the shadows and take away from any visibility there was.

I wouldn't wear headphones on that stretch of road even in the daytime — the trees muffle engine noises, and what with all the bends in the road you can't accurately hear cars coming; cars aside, a lot of that hewn-back cliff is held up with wire netting to protect from landslides, but they do happen, and you need to be able to hear them. Walking along the side of the road at that time of night, though, it was... eerie.

My breathing sounded so loud in my ears I felt like it could be heard for miles, and even the sound of my own heartbeat — there was no wind, no sound of cars in the distance, not even the trees creaking. Now and then, I'd hear an animal call like a gamebird or something, or hear a stick break in the underbrush down the valley side, and every time it made me jump a mile.

They say it's haunted, that stretch of road — but then, every road in Wales is probably haunted at some point, right? Every road anywhere. If we've been about for two hundred thousand years, there must be ghosts anywhere anybody's ever lived — because they've died there, too.

Fog had come in, was clinging to the edges of the valley side like skirts against someone's ankle, thick and white.

I don't believe in ghosts, and I didn't walking home that night, but it's the sort of thing you think about when you're trudging home in the middle of the night, when it's all deserted, when it's frighteningly quiet and you're shrouded in the night fog.

Every time I stepped into the blank space between two stretches of lamplight and was suddenly drenched in whiteness, I felt like I'd dropped into an ocean of the stuff, even though the next reach of the street light was only a few steps away and I could see it right ahead of me. I kept doing a stupid little run through the shadowed bits, feeling heat flush the back of my neck and a shiver run down my spine, and then I felt pissed off I'd even done that, because I was just making myself scared.

I knew when I'd reached the halfway point because there's a path that comes off the main road and leads about thirty or forty paces down to a public footpath, and I glanced down the hill to see if there were any cars parked there. The street lamp overlooking it was broken, so I couldn't see very well, but I couldn't see reflection off a windshield or a car light.

I hadn't heard any cars all night, or had any drive past me, which was all for the best. I had an old duffel coat on over the top of my dress, and it wasn't exactly high-vis.

I don't know why I thought there'd be cars parked down there at this time of night — even if there had been cars parked outside of the public woods, they'd only be doggers — but for some reason I was convinced there'd be somebody. I took a few steps off the main road, looking, certain I'd see something, that there had to be someone there.

It's weird, when you're looking for something in almost pitch-darkness and you're trying to make your eyes focus with not quite enough light to see by. I could see something. It was below the level of the fog, and at first, it was almost like I just saw something flit between the trees, and then when I stopped to stare, I could only see the trees themselves, their silhouette, but then it moved again.

I thought it was just a man at first, because I was staring right down the embankment and the shadow of him seemed to come out from behind one of the bigger oak trees, the really old ones that've been there longer than my granddad's been alive.

I nearly said hello, or said something, started to raise my hand, but it was like I was frozen with my breath caught in my throat as it got closer. It wasn't easy to judge the size of it because in the dark I couldn't actually tell the distance very easily, but the proportions were wrong, off. I could see the glint of its eyes too high up, and its head was bigger than its shoulders, the eyes too far apart, and it wasn't moving like it was walking, but just sort of... rising.

Getting closer.

It should have been making noise. There should have been twigs snapping, leaves rustling, dirt shifting, but there was nothing but ringing silence down there, beneath the fog.

I couldn't breathe, couldn't even move, didn't even dare blink with how it was coming closer, and I wanted to cry suddenly, wanted to scream, because I'd stepped off the path, hadn't I? I'd stepped out of the light and into the shadows and just like I was scared of there *was* something, it *was* wrong.

I didn't know what it was, could just see the shadow of it and hear my blood rushing in my ears, so rooted to the spot in terror I couldn't so much as shift my weight—

And then there was a hand on my shoulder, and I actually screamed.

I clapped my hand over my mouth, looking from the man in front of me to back down the hill, but when I looked this time, there was nothing there — no shadow, no big black thing, nothing.

"Sorry, sorry," he said anxiously — he had been wearing a flat cap, and now he had his hands in front of him and was passing it anxiously between them, turning it in circles. "I didn't mean to frighten you, Miss, I'm sorry. Just— You shouldn't be walking this road alone, Miss, just wanted to see you were alright."

I was shaking all over, huddled in my coat, and I kept looking from him down the hill, scanning for the figure, but it wasn't there.

"This land in't right, Miss," he said, and I looked at his face, trying to see if I recognised him, which I don't think I did. He had a pointy chin and a slightly upturned nose, freckles scattered on his round cheeks, and he had quite long eyelashes for a boy — they made him look like a boy when he wasn't, really, I think he must have actually been about my age, twenty-five, twenty-seven, because his voice was deep. "You don't want to be lingering on it. Can I give you a lift? Where are you going to?"

"Rhyd-gwyn," I said, and he nodded.

"I'm going through Rhyd, it's no trouble to stop to let you off," he said. "I can drop you home."

It was late, and I still had gooseflesh all over me, cold underneath my coat, and even as I was double-thinking it, getting into a car with some stranger I'd never seen before in the middle of the night, I was so freaked out I just followed him up to the road again.

I needn't have been worried: he wasn't driving a car.

I stood there, staring, at the big Welsh Cob harnessed to the cart behind it, a green-painted thing with a wooden bench on the front of it and a bunch of crates and sacks in the cart itself. The horse was bright white, not just the mane but its main coat, and I reached out to touch it, felt the heat radiating from it when I brushed my fingers over the side of its neck.

"Come on, brysiwch," he said as he hopped up onto the bench, settling back with the reins held in his hand. "This is wild country, this, off the road. This road isn't meant to be here, cut into the mountain as it is, and it knows it."

"What does that mean?" I asked as I stepped forward and pulled myself up onto the bench. He clicked his tongue and his mare started forward, her hooves making regular noise on the tarmac as she followed the lines of the road. "Wild country?"

He didn't say anything, looking forward on the path, and I was so stunned by the situation and still a little drunk I didn't say anything either, just sat there on the bench beside him, my hands folded in my lap and held between my knees. There was a lantern hung on one side of the bench's back, and I could feel the heat coming off of it.

He was dressed in a brown wool coat and had his cap back on his head, leather boots, grey trousers. It sounds ridiculous, I know, but despite everything, despite the whole situation, the outfit wasn't *that* far off to what some of the older farmers wear, and the cart was in good nick.

I'd never seen someone drive a cart on this road — I don't think I've ever seen someone drive a cart locally at all, except for farmer's fairs and the like.

"You live in Rhyd-gwyn?" he asked casually. I'm glad it was casual — I'm glad he was focused on the horse and the reins in his hands, and not on me.

"Behind the King's Swan," I told him. "Just off the main road."

"I know it, yeah."

"Where are you going?" I asked him, and he looked at me sideways, gave me a small, warm smile. There was something shy about it, I think.

"Oh, you know," he said, and shrugged his shoulders. "Home."

"Where's home?"

Just asking the question made me feel like I'd been plunged in cold water, and that was before he turned away and looked straight on again, the smile fading from his lips.

"A long ways yet," he said.

I tried to pay attention as we kept on moving, focused on the clip-clop of the mare's hooves on the tarmac, tried to focus on her and the way she almost seemed to fade into the thick, white mist around us, the fog the same colour as she was so that you couldn't really see where the horse ended and it started. If I hadn't touched her, if I hadn't actually felt her body under my hand, I might have believed he'd bridled the fog itself.

A few times, I looked off over the side of the path, staring into the darkness and looking to see if there was anything else down there, if there were any more shapes flitting between the trees, and the first few times I didn't see anything.

The third time — the fourth, maybe? — I saw a dark shape move on a path I knew led down to and crossed over a stream. It was smaller than the other one had been, but it moved fast, and once again, it made no noise at all, no snapping or rustling in the undergrowth beneath it.

My breath caught in my throat, and I gripped the arm of the cart bench to lean over and look, but the driver nudged me with his shoulder.

"Try not to," he advised me in an undertone, not taking his eyes off the road ahead for a moment. "Bessie's got blinders on, it's easy for her. We have to just not look."

"Not look," I repeated. "What did you — Wild country, you said. What do you mean by that?"

He looked at me sideways, his eyes slightly wide so that I saw the whites of them. "Best not to talk about it, Miss."

"I want to talk about it," I said. "You're the one who said it. Wild country, you called this. How's this wild country? This road's been cut through here for donkey's years — it's been here since the seventeen or eighteen hundreds when they started up the quarry. What do you mean by that, calling it wild country?"

"Well," he whispered, his voice so quiet I had to lean in to hear him. "You can cut through country like this, Miss, you can even cut into the mountain a bit. You can put in the road and you can pave it and you can line it with lamps and you can hold back the slides with stakes and boards. You can't live on it, can you? We can walk back and forth, ride through on a cart, but it's not really ours, it's not yours or mine, it's not owned by anybody. You can't tame country like this unless it wants to be tamed. It's still wild — especially on a night like this, can't see your hand in front of your face. A man could get lost on a night like this — many a man has."

I didn't say a word, couldn't even breathe in, and he glanced at me again and came over almost a little shy, said, "Or, or a woman, of course." He swallowed. "And if you did get lost, you wouldn't be able to find your way back, would you? Maybe if you made it down to the river, and it was the right one."

"I saw something," I said.

"Eh?"

"I saw something," I told him again. "In the dark, down the embankment, I don't know what it was, but it was, it was a shadow, it was getting so much closer when you—"

"Listen," he said, shifting in his seat. "Listen, like I said, Miss, best we don't talk about that." He flicked his wrist, moving the reins, and Bessie picked up her pace. "Best we don't talk at all, as it happens."

We didn't have that much farther to go, but the whole time my heart was pounding in my chest, and it only started to slow down when we came over the crest of the hill and I could see the lights of the village proper. There was barely any fog in town, only the barest hints of mist on the river and clinging around the bridge.

"Here we are," he said as we came down the main road, already past village hall and the church and the graveyard, and got Bessie to come to a stop.

I hopped down, looking to the sign for the Queen's Swan, Est. 1802, at the old painting of the swan on it that was faded now — the sign was a lot newer than the pub, obviously, was more like forty years old rather than two hundred. I turned back to thank him, and he was already gone, Bessie and the cart, too — not fading into the distance or carrying on down the street, but just... gone.

I nearly ran the two minutes up the path to home, had my phone torch on even though it was pretty well-lit, and there was no fog.

I didn't want to be alone in the dark for a second, and even when I got inside and upstairs and into bed, cosy under the covers so that I could finally go to sleep, it was with all the lights on.

FIN.

The Door

They forgot about the door, somehow.

When they moved into the house, it had been fascinating: a full-sized door in the hall between Dad's room and Kelly's, a door that would not open. For weeks, the girls rifled in the backs of drawers, peered under loose floorboards, dug in the yard.

They searched high and low for wherever one might find a key in an old house, and they even found one, but it was for the old iron padlock in the shed, that wasn't even keeping anything closed.

Mostly, they found screws, pennies, and bits of lint.

They tried to peek into the room, of course — it had an old-fashioned keyhole, but peering through it, one could only see a dark room (from the outside you could see the curtains were closed), and the crack underneath the door wasn't enough to push anything under.

Even when they pulled and dragged and pushed at the door's handle, it didn't even rattle in the frame.

The door remained closed. in due time, the girls forgot about it, and so did Dad.

It was part of the wall, almost, or might as well have been.

One day, someone asked Corah in class if there was anything interesting about her house, and she'd thought for a second before saying that they had a stained glass window in the attic bedroom, and that when you were up in the attic, it left colours staining the floor.

She didn't even remember the door until she came home, and then she looked at it, surprised.

Strange, how completely you can forget something you see every day.

Strange, how she forgot it again afterwards.

Dad died in September, and they stayed with Aunt Bea for a few days before she brought them back to the house, and Kelly didn't realise why Corah was stopped stock still on the landing, staring, until she got up the stairs herself.

"I forgot about that door," she whispered.

"So did I," said Corah, and reached for her sister's hand, squeezed it so tightly it hurt, but Kelly just squeezed right back. They were meant to be packing, but she couldn't move, rooted to the spot.

She felt very frightened. She didn't know why.

The door that they had forgotten — and how could they have forgotten it? It was right there! — was ajar. Inside the room, it was pitch dark, although the curtains looked the same as the ones in Kelly's room from the outside, and they didn't keep out light at all.

No, in the room they had forgotten, it was very dark indeed. They were still dressed in the clothes they'd worn at the funeral this morning. Corah still had tears stained on her cheeks.

The door creaked further open, as though someone were slowly pushing it.

It was still very dark inside, as dark as the cellar got when the light was off and you had the door closed, and it didn't feel like that should be possible.

They had seen the gaps in the curtains, after all. They'd talked about looking in with a ladder.

They never had. They'd forgotten, hadn't they? How had they forgotten?

Aunt Bea was calling them from downstairs, but neither of them really heard.

In the dark, Dad said, "I've missed you, girls. Why don't you come give your daddy a hug?"

FIN.

The Coffin at Sea

A vessel picks up a coffin afloat at sea.

It's heavy, and the captain orders that they open it to see if there are any identifying features, so they know to whom they should return it — no nails hold it shut, and it opens easily.

The bed is dry, but empty.

Unnerved but in many ways relieved, the sailors toss it back.

That night, the alarm is raised when it appears on deck again, silently, with no trace of who had brought it back aboard.

The empty bed beckons.

The sailors toss it overboard again, this time heavy with ballast.

It reappears: the ballast is gone.

The empty bed beckons.

The sailors begin to get into their heads the idea that this cursed box will not leave them until one of their number is laid to rest inside it.

One of the riggers, a japester, lays himself in the bed as his friend pushes it over the side: it is a bright morning in shallow waters, and it should be impossible to lose sight of him for even a moment.

The coffin disappears.

The rigger is not seen again.

That night, the coffin reappears on the central deck, leaned against the foremast, upright this time.

Its empty bed beckons.

FIN.

The Ring

He puts the flowers on the bed of Marcus' grave which was grown over with grass now. Except for a slight roundness to the earth, a change in level between the ground and the grave grown over with grass, you might believe no one was buried there at all.

But Marcus was there, of course.

Six feet beneath him, laid back in the coffin in the nicest of his suits, the one with the blue-and-green checked waistcoat to match the lining of his suit jacket.

No tie.

Marcus always hated wearing ties.

He'd worn his father's old ring, too, which he never took off even though he'd hated his father — he'd worn it out of spite, knowing the old man would hate that he had it on him, and because he liked the weight it added to a punch.

Rein had used to play over the polished stone in it with his thumb at night.

It was threatening to rain but nothing had come down yet so Rein stood at the gravesite with his umbrella loosely held against his thigh staring down at the headstone that read **MARCUS GRISHAM-WATFORD, LOVING BROTHER AND DEVOTED PARTNER.**

His mother hadn't wanted that last bit on the headstone, but she didn't have any control over it and Marcus had made sure in his will that was the case — Toni, Marcus' sister, had insisted on it, on having Rein and their relationship mentioned, even though Rein had said it was okay, that it shouldn't be there, if it was causing so much upset.

Rein appreciated it, the effort. The care.

His memories of Marcus were starting to fade, which made him ache in a tired, hollow way. He couldn't remember the way Marcus used to smell, the honeyed, woody scent of him, and he was starting to forget how it had felt when Marcus held him back against his breast.

It was all fading, just like Marcus had.

Rein wondered if his memories were rotting away with the body beneath his feet, if as soon as Marcus himself was bare bones picked clean by bugs and worms, he'd be left only with the memories to fit them.

It was cold, but he didn't feel ready to move just yet. He knew it wouldn't change anything, knew that staying rooted to the spot staring down at a gravestone wouldn't make Marcus come home, wouldn't make him feel better, wouldn't matter. Ryan hated it when he got like this, when he got stuck and he wouldn't move on, when he was like a lingering ghost instead of a real person.

He just wasn't ready yet.

* * *

An hour later, on the bus home, he was shivering a little from the cold and the wet — it had started to rain and that had convinced his feet to move — and his phone rang. He was slow and clumsy pulling it out, his fingers stiff, a few drips of wetness on the screen, and dread bubbled in his belly the more seconds ticked by, the longer he took.

"Hi, Ryan," he said softly once he had the phone up to his ear.

"Where are you?" Ryan asked sharply.

"On the bus. I'm coming home."

"On another walk, were you?"

"Yes."

Rein could almost imagine Ryan softening as he heard him sigh. "I'll have something ready for you to eat," he said quietly. "And I'll make a hot water bottle for you."

"Thank you," Rein said, something twisting in the base of his gut. "I know I don't deserve it."

Ryan clucked his tongue, and hung up the phone.

When he got home, Ryan held his arms out for him, and Rein fell between his spread knees onto the sofa, falling against his chest and relaxing as Ryan wrapped his arms around him, squeezing him tightly.

One hand wound up into Rein's hair, the other hand settling possessively on his arse.

"Were you at his grave again?" asked Ryan softly, his breath hot on the shell of Rein's ear, and Rein closed his eyes, leaning in closer, pressing his face against the heat of Ryan's chest. "Christ, Rein."

Rein liked the way Ryan said his name. Some people said "Rein" the same way they said Ryan's, or said to rhyme with shine, or sometimes people asked if he liked kings or the monarchy, if it was like reign.

"I'm sorry," said Rein. "I know you don't like it."

"It's not that I don't like it, sweetheart, it just hurts for you to keep feeling bad over him when he treated you so badly." Ryan stroked his back in a slow, rhythmic fashion, his palm moving up and down, up and down. "He still has power over you even now."

"It's not power," said Rein. "I can be sad he's gone."

"Are you sad he doesn't lose his temper all the time anymore, throw stuff at the walls whenever something pisses him off? Scared he doesn't punch the fuck out of any guy that looks at you anymore?"

Rein gently traced the scar on Ryan's shoulder where it adjoined his neck — he remembered the crack his nose had made when Marcus had punched him, and the way Ryan had sailed backward, how he'd fell into the wire potto basket in the kitchen. It had almost seemed animated, or as if it was in slow motion, the movement had been so obvious and so dramatic — there'd been so much blood, afterward, Rein was sure he'd die.

Marcus had stormed out as Rein had called the ambulance, and he'd been so panicked he hadn't even pulled his clothes back on, had still been naked except for Ryan's blood when the ambulance arrived.

They'd thought he was hurt too, but he wasn't. Marcus never hit him, not once, never hurt him even by accident. He couldn't hurt Rein, he said — Rein was too precious. That annoyed Ryan, Rein thought, in the scheme of things. It would have been easier if Marcus had hit him.

He remembered how upset he'd been when Ryan insisted on pressing charges, even though they were in Marcus' kitchen, Marcus' flat, Marcus' bed. Ryan had said the lease was in Rein's name and he had the right to do what he wanted, but—

It was his fault.

All of it was his fault. It didn't matter that Ryan said otherwise — it was his fault. He'd been lonely, sometimes, what with the hours Marcus worked and how unpredictable they were, and it had seemed safer, somehow, easier, to let Ryan come closer, than to ask Marcus to come home more. It had seemed easy to let Ryan kiss his neck and slide his fingers under his waistband, to let Ryan creep into his life and his affections.

If he hadn't — if he'd told Ryan no, if he told Marcus he missed him even when they were sitting together, if he'd told Marcus it frightened him sometimes, when he raised his voice, if he'd just said —

He wouldn't have fought Ryan. He wouldn't have run, afterward, and no one would have chased him.

He wouldn't have died.

He thought. Maybe.

"You know no one loves you like I do, right, sweetheart?" Ryan asked, his voice soft in Rein's ear, but his grip was a little too tight around his wrist, but he couldn't say so, because Ryan got upset if he said things like that. He said it made him sound like he was as bad as Marcus was. "You know I always loved you more than he did?"

Rein let himself be repositioned like a puppet in Ryan's lap, let Ryan slowly rock his hips up against his arse, sighed, leaned back against him.

"If I didn't care about you, I wouldn't have risked it," he said softly, grazing his teeth over the lobe of Rein's ear and making him shiver.

"Thank you," Rein whispered.

"Going to show me you love me?"

"I love you."

"Going to show me?"

Marcus had never made him do this, had never asked after the first time he'd tried and choked on it.

Rein slipped onto the rug and knelt between Ryan's knees.

* * *

"Other people think you're broken," said Ryan that night, spooned up behind him, and it made Rein's stomach twist, something clenching inside him. "Because you never react to anything, because you're so blank. But I know you're not, baby — I understand you."

The clenching discomfort morphed into a delicate warmth, one that felt tender and fragile. He pressed back against the muscular bulk of Ryan's body, encouraging him to squeeze his arms more tightly around his waist.

"I'm not broken," he said.

"I know," Ryan assured him, kissing his neck. "I'm not like everyone else, I never thought you were."

Rein was awake for hours later, held in Ryan's arms. It took him ages to fall asleep.

* * *

He found it in a box of Marcus' old things.

Ryan had been quick about throwing most of it out, saying that Rein didn't need that sort of negativity in his life, and he'd weakly objected, but what would he have done with it all, anyway?

He'd never been as cultured as Marcus was — Toni had taken his books and his suits and his little busts, and Ryan had thrown the rest out. This was in the back of the wardrobe, where Ryan hadn't looked just yet.

He stayed over a lot, recently. The flat was Rein's now, without Marcus in it, but sometimes, he felt like it was Ryan's. He felt like he was Ryan's, except for the times that he wasn't.

The box in the back of the wardrobe was full of trophies and medals — Marcus had done sports at school. He'd been a runner and he'd played tennis, and he'd done team sports too. It had always seemed somewhat unfair that he was so good at sports and at academics at the same time when Rein had never been much good at anything.

One of the trophies was for some sort of university quiz, and Rein stroked over the text carved into the metal, feeling the cool texture of it. He'd wanted to display them, put them up on nice shelves, but Marcus had laughed at the suggestion.

"No, Rein," he'd said, kissing his cheek. "I don't think we need to tell everyone how fast or smart I was as a kid. It's old news, not impressive."

"I wasn't smart as a kid, or fast. It's impressive to me."

"You're smart now."

"I don't have a medal."

"I'll get you one."

Rein reached up, absently wiping the tears that had formed at the corner of his eyes. He'd have to hide the box until he could give it to Toni — he didn't want Ryan to throw it away, but Toni understood. She never blamed Rein, even though perhaps she should.

At the side of the box was a wide board, and he thought it was another plaque until he pulled it out and turned it over. The alphabet was spread over the wooden surface, painted on in ornate, dark letters, with YES, NO, HELLO, and GOODBYE at the corners.

He'd never liked the Ouija board. He remembered the first time he'd seen it. Marcus had seen his face and his fear, had teased once, and when Rein had very seriously shook his head, he'd promised never to touch it again. Rein hadn't seen it since.

Here it was, in the back of the wardrobe.

A fresh wave of guilt ran through him as he reached into the box for the planchette.

It had a shirtless demon drawn on it, with a visible bulge in his boxers. For all the fear building up inside him, it made him smile. Marcus had been good at lots of things, but drawing he hadn't been quite as good at — the demon's eyes were lopsided and its face didn't look quite right.

Ryan wouldn't be home from his shift for another few hours.

Rein had time.

He closed the blinds and turned on the desk lamp instead of the ceiling light, and sat down with the planchette on the board. He moved it slowly, circling it on the board, feeling how easily it rolled.

"Is anybody there?" he asked, feeling the hair stand up on the back of his neck, embarrassed and scared all at once. He kept slowly rolling the planchette in easy circles, feeling no tug or pull or catch, wondering if he was an idiot for expecting it.

"Hello?" he asked.

The sound of it was soothing, rhythmic.

"Marcus?" he asked in a tiny voice. "Marcus?"

The planchette stuck, and Rein felt like he'd been drenched in ice water.

Rein looked down at the board and read the word the planchette pointed to: **HELLO.**

He burst into tears in earnest, this time.

"Marcus," he said softly. "Is it you?"

The planchette tugged his fingers as it slit to the word **YES**. Rein sniffled, and the planchette moved fast, his fingers barely touching the wood as it slid one way and then the other: **DONT CRY**.

"Sorry," he whispered, and he bit his lip, hearing a creak in the corridor and thinking it was Ryan, but it wasn't. Just a neighbour in the hall.

"Are you — Are you okay?"

MISS YOU, said the planchette, letter by letter. Rein's chest ached, his whole body ached. **NEED YOU**.

"Need me?"

YOUR HELP.

Rein paused, his lips falling apart. "What with?"

MY RING.

Rein stared down at the board, feeling baffled, suspended in a sea of confusion, as he tried to think.

"Your — Your ring? Your dad's ring? But, Marcus, you were buried with it, I can't just—"

The planchette moved fast enough to make a louder sound on the board, a sort of sharp scraping. It wasn't the same as a real shout, but it still made him flinch back, and when he opened his eyes again, he saw the planchette hovering over the word **NO**.

"You were," he said. "I remember, you were—"

WAS I?

Doubt flooded his brain. He felt like he was swimming in it.

"You were," Rein said slowly, wanting to pull his hands into his lap and make himself smaller, to curl in on himself, but he didn't dare pull his hands away from the planchette. "You were," he said again, more softly. "You were, because me and Toni talked about it, and your mu—"

The planchette moved fast, and even counting out the letters, he felt as though he could hear Marcus' tone, hear the dark and dangerous way he would talk sometimes, the way that made Rein want to fold back into his own bones.

YOU THINK IM LYING?

Rein's eyes watered.

"No," Rein said quickly when he realised he'd been quiet for too long, trying not to sniffle as though Marcus wouldn't know if he couldn't hear him cry. "No, no, I'm not saying that, but I remember, I remember how it looked wh—"

6 MONTHS AGO?

"Yeah, but—"

YOU SURE?

Rein felt himself crumple, and the planchette made circle after circle around the board before coming back to the question mark, again and again. It reminded him of how Marcus would tug open a cupboard door sometimes and keep letting it drop back against its magnet before tugging it open again.

He'd do that when he was impatient and was trying not to be angry, when Rein was taking too long and being too slow and too stupid, and it made him feel as though he were about to explode, too much pressure on his too-full skull.

"I'm sorry," Rein said thickly, loudly, because he just wanted it to stop, and when the planchette stopped moving he almost sobbed with relief.

GET MY RING, said the planchette.

Rein swallowed.

PLEASE?

Rein swallowed again, throat feeling too full, and nodded his head.

The planchette turned in his hand to point the way, and he very carefully put the board and the box back into the wardrobe, kicking it to the back before he pulled on his coat. The planchette shifted in his hand, impatient, and he held it in a loose grip as he stepped outside.

They'd made him identify the body.

Antonia had been up in Aberdeen, hadn't come back down south yet, and so they'd made him come because they weren't married but they were each other's next of kin and all the pigs knew Rein by sight even though they'd never arrested him. He and Marcus had been in each other's wills even though Rein had nothing to leave behind.

It had been horrible, seeing him. He'd gone down to the train lines, was probably walking out to the woods like he always did, and Ryan had told the police that even though Rein had said not to, and Ryan had left a bruise, shoving him back from the door to keep him from going out to find Marcus first.

Not on purpose.

He'd been stressed out about the police coming to take another statement, because he'd had to have stitches at the hospital and was hazy from the drugs, and he hadn't even realised until later, then he'd kissed the mark on Rein's chest.

Rein knew it wasn't on purpose — it was Rein's fault, Ryan had said once, because he had such delicate skin, because he bruised so easily.

Marcus had been twice Ryan's size, and he'd never even left a bruise during sex.

He'd looked very cold laid out on the mortuary bed. He'd been scaling a chain link fence, one that Rein knew he knew a way around but it was a half mile up the line and he was probably in a hurry to get up and over, to make sure they couldn't catch up.

They said he'd hit his head falling over the other side. Instant. Quick.

It hadn't looked so quick on that metal table, under the blue-white lights and the reflection off the dark green tiles. His skull had been smashed, he'd landed right on a rock, and it had looked—

The planchette tugged him back, hard: he'd crossed into the road without thinking and a food truck roared past him, leaving him standing on the curb, breathing heavily as he tried to catch his focus back. The planchette felt warm in his hand, and he wished he remembered what Marcus' hand felt like.

He held it up to his chest for a second, hugging it against him as he waited for the traffic lights to change, and then he crossed the road, glancing down at his boots as he made his way forward.

Marcus had bought them for him. He'd said that last week, that Marcus had bought them for him specially and that was why they fitted so well, and Ryan had let out an irritated sound and walked out of the room.

He didn't think he was broken. He just put up with things he shouldn't sometimes.

Rein was a forgiving person — Ryan said that, that he was a forgiving person, too forgiving, but he'd never quite understood who Ryan wanted him to forgive and who he didn't, because he always seemed to get it wrong.

It was easier to let Ryan decide.

His boots squelched in the mud as he walked down the dirt path toward the train tracks, their wide bend before the track caught up with the station, although they passed through a little valley cut into the hillside first, stabilised with brick on each side.

When they were teenagers, it used to be that they'd slide down the bricked-up bank on damp days, sitting on the back of a tray, and Rein was always frightened to do it himself — Marcus would always go down first and catch him when he skidded to the bottom, lift him up into a kiss.

It used to dazzle him in those days, and for a second he stood at the top of the tall bank, looking down at the rail track on the bottom. This was a utility trail, really, the stairs leading down for tunnel access — there was a proper path further away — but this was a shortcut.

A sign read **DANGER — KEEP OUT**, but the gate wasn't very high, was barely a stile to hop over. The planchette tugged him forward, and as his feet dropped down onto the topmost metal panel of the stairs, he smelt a woody, vanilla scent, smelt Marcus, and lingered.

It encompassed him in a cloud, made him close his eyes and hover for a moment, and holding the planchette to his chest he imagined Marcus was with him, arms wrapped around him, smelling his cologne—

His phone rang.

"Hi, baby," Ryan said when he answered. There was a slightly stiff note to his voice, and Rein pulled the planchette closer to his chest, as if Ryan could see it. "Where are you?"

"Just walking," said Rein. "I needed to get out of the house."

"You at the graveyard again? Jesus, Rein—"

"No."

"Are you fucking lying to me? It's bad enough you want to worship your dead ex, but to then—"

"I'm not lying," Rein said. "I'm not at the graveyard. I'm going to the woods, I'm just at the train tracks."

He heard Ryan exhale.

"I'm sorry," he said. "I know I get angry sometimes, that it's not fair. I'm sorry, baby, I didn't mean it. I just — I get so angry, thinking about how he hurt you. You understand that, don't you?"

He wasn't my ex, Rein doesn't say. *I didn't want him to be my ex.*

"Yes."

"You know I love you, that I want to protect you?"

"Yes."

Rein could smell Marcus' cologne, and the air felt warm although the day was cool, and the planchette was a hot weight on his chest, against his palm.

"I'll drive over to you," said Ryan.

The planchette jumped in his palm, and he squeezed it hard to keep it still.

"Okay," he said quietly in a small, tight voice. "In — In ten minutes, fifteen? I'll make it there. To the other side."

"I can walk with you, just give me—"

"No, it's so muddy, Ryan," Rein said, forcing himself to smile so that Ryan could hear it in his voice. "I don't want you to ruin your shoes. Meet me on the path in the woods, it's okay."

A beat passed.

"Okay," said Ryan. "I'll meet you in five."

"Uh, I'll be ten, I think, maybe—"

"Five."

"... Okay."

He hung up the phone and moved quickly on the stairs, gripping tightly against the steel railing, because he remembered when they'd been kids and Chloe J had slipped on the metal plate while it was wet, the corrugation making no difference at all, and had sprained her wrist.

He wondered if Marcus would have been okay, if he'd slipped here instead of going over the chain link. It would rain soon, he thought, and the plate would be even wetter.

The planchette pulled him forward, on along, and he stepped carefully between the wooden slats of the tracks. They seemed so small, now — still big, of course, big enough for the train, and he knew not to touch the metal sides in case he electrocuted himself, but they'd seemed so much bigger when he was young.

The tunnel loomed ahead of him, a dark and hungry mouth.

The planchette suddenly stopped feeling like anything, and he paused, distress rippling through his body as he thought Marcus had abandoned him again, but then he saw the little stone beside the track, saw the shine of the ring.

The stone wasn't even broken, although the ring was muddied and wet with rainwater and the silver was starting to tarnish. He felt as though something had been torn out of him as he dropped to his knees to pick it up.

Rain was beginning to come down in fat, heavy drops, landing on his shoulders.

Marcus had been telling the truth, then. Rein had misremembered, had been stupid again just like always, and he felt so guilty and so pained, like a part had been torn out of him. Kneeling there with the rain rushing down on him and sinking in against his skin, he polished the ring with the sleeve of his hoodie, trying to clean it off.

Marcus' arms were warm around him, squeezing him tight like they always used to, and he couldn't see them, but he could feel Marcus' hands over his, gently squeezing his wrists as he turned the ring over.

"I'm sorry," Rein whispered. "I'm sorry, I'll put it on your grave—"

"You wanted something to remember me by, didn't you?" Marcus asked in his ear, and Rein felt safer than he'd ever known, felt like crying, felt like he was about to fall to pieces. "Do you remember me now?"

Rein, teary-eyed — or maybe it was just the rain — nodded his head, squeezed the metal in his fingers.

"It's not a medal," said Marcus. "I'm sorry it's not a medal, I know you wanted one—"

Through the tears, Rein nodded his head, breath hitching, gasping.

"He take care of you?" asked Marcus, voice lower, darker. "He take care of what's mine?"

It felt like a trap.

"Not like you do," whispered Rein, hoping this was the right answer: he was rewarded by a tight squeeze, but not one so tight it was painful, and he wondered if Marcus' cologne would catch on his skin, if Ryan would be able to smell it on him. It was still a sore point, and he had no one else to tell — maybe that was why he said, "He said I'm broken."

"You're not broken," said Marcus immediately.

"He said people think I am."

"No, no one thinks you're broken," said Marcus. "They just think you're kind — too kind for your own good, maybe, but not broken. There's nothing wrong with you. Never has been, I promise."

He kissed Rein's temple and Rein closed his eyes, leaning into him. "Did it hurt?"

"No, not really. I was drunk, and I think it killed me as soon as I hit the floor." His voice was quiet, gentle. Rumbling like an affectionate bear. "I just hurt because I was missing you, thought you hated me."

"I didn't hate you," Rein said, his own voice choked and sharp and ugly, but Marcus stroked his hands. "I didn't hate you, I just — It was just hard to talk to you sometimes. To tell you things. It was easy to talk to Ryan, he's just, he was better at it, at talking."

"Good at other things too," rumbled Marcus, and Rein's breath hitched, but Marcus hushed him. "No, Rein, I'm not angry at you, I'm not having a go, I swear. But you never have to do anything you don't want to, you know. Don't have to suck him off, don't have to go to his work drinks when the women there treat you like you're his pet chihuahua or their gay best friend."

Marcus was stroking up and down his wrists, thumbs sliding smooth over the skin, and it was comforting, gentle, even though the rain was cold.

"You can call Toni if you need help getting out. You know that, right?"

"Yes."

"But you don't want to."

Rein bit his lip.

"It's okay if you want to stay with him," said Marcus. "I just want you happy, baby."

"No one else would want me. And Ryan loves me, he says he loves me—"

"Of course someone else would want you," Marcus whispered. "Don't you see how precious you are?"

"It would be hard to go. To leave. I don't know how."

"You don't know how? Rein, all you need to do—"

"I just want it to go back to the way it was," Rein blurted out, gasping in a breath, pressing his cheek hard against Marcus' shoulder, the shoulder he couldn't see. "I miss it. I miss you. It's all my fault, I should never have..."

Marcus squeezed him even tighter, so tight he almost couldn't breathe for a moment, but then Marcus relaxed his hold.

"I love you," he said. "You know I love you, don't you?"

"I love you too."

"Yeah," said Marcus. "Yeah, I know."

The rain seemed very loud, and Rein wondered if it would storm later, if the sky would split apart with thunder and lightning. He could barely see when he opened his eyes, the rain was coming down so heavy, and he was soaked to his skin.

"Rein!" shouted Ryan, and he looked up.

He could barely see him except for the tall lamp up behind him, frantically waving his arms, and Rein winced and put his finger in one of his ears at the loud roar of the rain, squinting up at him.

"Rein, baby, come here, come up here," Ryan shouted.

"No, it's okay!" Rein called back as he stood up, the planchette dropping to the ground, and held up the ring. "I have Marcus'—" He stared at the band of plain, rusted steel in his hand, a ring-pull off a can or maybe a keyring once, now too rusted to tell.

"Oh," he said lowly, feeling confused, his head all full, his brain spinning in his skull He'd just been holding it, the ring, hadn't it? He'd held it and the stone had been so polished, and —

"Rein, baby, get off the tracks," screamed Ryan, too loud through the cotton wool stuffed in his ears and behind his eyes. "Rein, just come here, just come up—"

The train was so loud, and its light was too bright as it came through the thick curtains of rain, and he put his arm over his eyes to shield them.

It happened quickly, and then it was done.

* * *

Marcus picked him up, and this time Rein could see him, feel him, touch him, smell his cologne.

"I have you, I have you," Marcus said, catching him in a kiss. It was tender, and he had to bend over to do it, to reach. "Don't cry, why are you crying? I hate it when you cry."

"That was wrong of you," said Rein, heaving in a sharp, shuddered gasp. "You made me feel crazy, I hate when you make me feel crazy, it's why I never told you things, it's why—"

"No, no, you asked for it," Marcus told him, cupping his cheeks. "Didn't you? Didn't you say you wanted it like before?" Marcus' thumbs slid through the tears and despite it all, Rein felt a crushing, painful relief.

He fell against Marcus' chest, and Marcus kissed him.

"You're mine, Rein," Marcus whispered. "You think I'd let dying change that?"

Rein shook his head, and Marcus held him.

"Can get a tray," he whispered against the top of Rein's head. "Or something like it. Run down that old hill like we used to."

"You have to catch me."

"It's not like you'll get hurt."

"Catch me anyway."

Marcus sighed, but leaned back, cupping Rein's cheek in one big, meaty hand. Rein could feel the weight of his ring against his skin, and he leaned into it.

"Always," Marcus promised. "Always."

FIN.

Green Thumb

Jacob's trade, in actuality, is handyman, but he does all sorts in and around the area, uses the skills his parents had given him.

His father had been a carpenter before he'd died, and his mother had been a prize-winning gardener in the area for years until she'd gone with her second husband to live in Cornwall a few years ago.

Jacob hardly minds that that's what she wants to do — she'd been so apologetic going, worrying about him running the farm by himself, but they've only ever had a small plot, and he's never had trouble keeping track of the chickens himself. She was getting on and on in her years, nearly seventy when she'd met Hamish after nine years widowed, and the work had been wearing on her enough that he was really quite glad she'd be so far away and no longer feel obligated to help when it was increasingly beyond her ability.

Apart from keeping track of the girls and setting their eggs along the road to sell at the Barnsleys' farm shop, he does all manner of things in and around Chesterton town — apart from his own garden, where he's won a few ribbons for his own rose varieties apart from his mother's own awards, he does the beds outside the village library, he does the flowers in Burnleigh's central square, and he always wins this or that at the annual festivals — for his flowers or for his bramble jams, occasionally for flower-arranging, although he doesn't do that sort of thing too often.

He likes to keep busy, is the thing, and so he's often doing this or that and getting paid for it, mending fences, helping people repair their rooves or their sheds or help with this or that on other people's farms, minding things for them when people are away.

The new neighbour is called Piers Hoult, and he lives about a mile down the road just on the edge of the village proper in a nice, fancy little cottage that had used to belong to Mr and Mrs Steele, before

Mr Steele had died, and Mrs Steele had gone to live in some sort of residential home close to their grandchildren in the city.

He comes over from said cottage, The Daisies, one Monday morning on foot — he doesn't drive, and when he goes into the city, he rides an old-fashioned bicycle — and knocks on Jacob's door, stands on his doorstep.

He's very pretty, except that Jacob feels that word catch in his head like it's not the right sort of word — Piers Hoult is undoubtedly *handsome*, isn't particularly feminine or girlish-looking or any of that, but he's... He's beautiful, is what he is. He's got big, dark brown eyes that glint in the morning sunshine, his hair thick, dark, and glossy, and his lips are carved into a perfect cupid's bow, and his skin is a sort of creamy white colour, shined almost to a polish.

"I'm so sorry to bother you, Mr Raine," he says, wringing delicate hands with beautiful pink nails that have been buffed to a shine. He's got a very soft voice, barely more than a whisper, but it's warm and honeyed, sweet. "I'm sure you're terribly busy, as ever — but would you have any time in the week, do you think, to give me some tips for gardening and that sort of thing?"

"Gardening?" repeats Jacob, drying his hands off on the towel he keeps in the hall, still wet with suds from the washing up.

"I've been trying desperately to grow some flowers," says Piers in his warm, quiet voice. "And I'm having no luck at all."

The Daisies is mostly stonework in the back and front garden — the Steeles had never been much for gardening.

"Of course, I can help," he says immediately, unable to hold back the immediate assent. "Let me grab my coat."

Piers Hoult, he decides in the coming weeks, is cursed.

There's nothing wrong with his fucking soil, that's for certain — the Daisies isn't far from Jacob's farm, and even if it *was* the soil, any sort of compost in pots Jacob brings around doesn't seem to do anything. He fills in the flowerbeds that the Steeles had just had pebbles in, and nothing grows in the earth; he tries to put in pots, and that doesn't work either.

He grows flowers at home in pots and brings those over, but when he comes back two days later, they're already dead and wilted in their earth.

"You must think I'm poisoning them," says Piers miserably, and Jacob assures him, "No, no, of course not!" although privately, he had been thinking that.

But even if he *had* been putting some sort of poison in the pots, he couldn't possibly be poisoning everything in the garden, too.

"Do you think it's my fault?" asks Piers, his eyes wide as dinnerplates. "Is it something wrong with me?"

"No," says Jacob. "*No.*"

Piers keeps looking at him, his eyes not quite as wide, his voice barely more than a whisper as he asks, "Are you sure?"

Something about it makes Jacob's hair stand on end, the back of his neck feeling prickly, a shiver running down his spine.

* * *

Jacob keeps trying.

He tries everything he can — seed trays where the soil stays barren for weeks on end no matter how carefully he coaxes the seedlings to come up; bringing cuttings over, or ready-grown seedlings over that wilt overnight if not before his eyes; *bouquets* wither within hours.

He brings over a yucca and it takes four days, but bit by bit, he really does watch it die. Before his eyes on day four, already having begun to darken, it dies off entirely, each long, spiky leaf turning brown at the base and yellow at the tip, wilting down and flopping against the trunk, some of them falling off in dead pieces.

It's late in the evening, and he'd been working all day before coming around here, so exhausted he could cry even though it's not even eight yet.

"Let me get you a cup of tea," says Piers, his hand cold and making his body jolt when it lands between his shoulders. He nudges Jacob into the living room, pushing him to sit down on his very plush, antique sofa, the only green thing in the house that won't fucking die. He slides his palm back and forth over the fabric, looking blearily at the back of the sofa, at its arms. There's something about it that's just...

"How old is this?" he asks as Piers pads out of the room, slowly lying down and putting his cheek against the arm, feeling how plush it is. His eyelids are desperately heavy, and he can't keep his eyes open, but the sofa feels wonderful. It smells faintly of something floral — lavender, he thinks.

"Oh, I don't know," Piers' voice drifts in from the kitchen. "I bought it in 1887, I think."

In retrospect, he's pretty sure he dreamed that: he's embarrassed as anything, but he's asleep before Piers comes back.

He'd been up since four o'clock, helping with the lambing at the Barnsleys' across the way before spending all day getting the flowers done in the big park, and then he'd been working in his own garden and tending the girls, and by the time he'd come over to Piers' he'd been tired to his bones, but that was no excuse for *this*.

It's one or so in the morning when he wakes, sitting up sharply.

The nice, fancy living room with all its antique and beautiful furniture that Jacob feels a bit too common to be allowed to be inside is dark, and there's no sign of Piers himself — he has a splitting headache and his shoulders ache, a glass of water on the coffee table beside him, a blanket over his shoulders.

He's embarrassed to face up to him, intends to avoids the other man for a few days — it's bad enough not to be able to do so much as grow the man a weed, but falling asleep on his fancy sofa still wearing his muck-covered work jeans is humiliating.

The door is unlocked when he leaves.

* * *

He trudges the mile home and sleeps in his own bed, and he's been awake for a few hours when Piers shows up on his doorstep.

"I'm so sorry, Jacob," he says, holding a plate of what and smell like fresh-baked pastries, offering out the plate. He's taking one before he can stop himself, mumbling a thank you. "I know I oughtn't have left you there, but you just looked so tired—"

"Oh, no, don't, don't worry about it," he says, because if anyone should be fucking apologising, it's *him*.

He's biting into the croissant, almost moans aloud at the taste of it, chocolate and something else, and he nearly chokes on it when Piers reaches out to play with the zip on Jacob's dungarees.

He doesn't know what to say about it, what to do, about Piers' handsome fingers with their impeccably pink nailbeds and their perfectly clean and buffed nails reaching across the gap between them, stroking over the corduroy and making sure the zip of his pocket sits flat.

"I wonder what people thought," says Piers idly, interrupting him before Jacob can tell him, desperate to tell him *something*, that these dungarees had been his father's. "Seeing you rush out of my home at so early an hour."

Jacob gulps down his mouthful of croissant, and Piers' smirk grows just a little wider.

"I wouldn't, um, presume—"

"What are you presuming?" asks Piers, raising his eyebrows and letting one of his fingers curl just under one of the straps of his dungarees. "I'm always terribly happy to have a strong, handsome man in my home."

When Piers leaves, Jacob is left almost swaying, watching the slight swing of Piers' arse as he departs.

* * *

He doesn't try at growing anything else at Piers' for a little while, focusing on preparing some of his vegetables for the next few months, the prize-winners in his greenhouse. He wonders if a greenhouse would help at Piers', even just a little plastic one on his garden table, although it probably wouldn't.

When Piers invites him for dinner, he brings a bouquet of cut flowers, some of his own and his mother's roses mixed together — in truth, he's probably more proud of his turnips than he is his roses, but Piers doesn't eat them.

He'd told Jacob that like it was a terrible secret, whispered it with one finger over his lips, apologetic, almost ashamed — "I don't eat turnips, Jacob. I don't eat carrots or potatoes, either."

He eats meat, certainly.

Jacob is too shy to say the steak Piers has cooked him is a little rare for his taste, especially because Piers eats his own blue, bluer than blue, and there's a streak of blood on his plate.

A little shines on his lower lip as they eat, and as Jacob watches, stunned and enchanted, Piers slides his thumb slowly through the redness before sucking it from his skin.

"You don't eat much meat, do you?" asks Piers, cocking his head to one side. "Me, I'm an abject carnivore."

Jacob shivers.

When Piers kisses him an hour later, Jacob almost expects to fall to the ground, he's so dizzy with it, but Piers doesn't taste like blood, which Jacob had expected.

Jacob staggers home feeling like he's drunk even though he barely had any of the wine Piers had poured him, and almost isn't upset that the roses he'd brought are already brown.

* * *

Piers visits Jacob's garden now and then, visits the park and the library and the central square in Burnleigh, wherever it is that Jacob's working, sits on benches and basks in the sun or reads his books. He's pretty well-off, as far as Jacob knows, but he honestly doesn't have an idea what the man actually does for his money.

It seems rude to ask.

It especially seems rude to ask when Piers says that he likes to watch Jacob work, and when Jacob so enjoys Piers enjoying him working — whenever Jacob, sweating, comes up to him, Piers always tugs him into a kiss, like now.

His mouth is slightly open, so that when Piers comes in to kiss him he almost sucks on the side of his jaw, and drags his tongue through the sweat shining there.

Jacob's knees go weak and he's laughing, but Piers catches him before he can fall, surprisingly strong for being such a beautiful, delicately built man.

He eats dinner with Piers again, and after they're done eating, Jacob pulls his surprise out of the basket he'd been keeping it hidden in: a plant pot filled with compost.

"It's empty," says Piers, pouting.

"It'll sprout," promises Jacob. "You're going to put it somewhere, and I'll come every day to tend it until it does."

Piers smiles, and his white teeth seem so sharp for a second, glinting in the light, when he pulls Jacob into the next kiss. "I know just where to put it," he murmurs against his mouth, and leads Jacob up the stairs by his wrist.

He indicates the bedside table, says, "Just here."

His bed is a large, comfortable-looking thing, so plush it seems like you might sink right into it, and it has red silk sheets and a canopy and golden-tasselled ties around its four posts, and as soon as Jacob puts the pot down, he's shoved down onto this bed on his back.

Piers' kiss, this time, is more than a dizzying thing: it's hungry, overpowering, and Jacob's heart is pounding hard in his chest, his lungs aching with how hard and heavy he's breathing, how the peaks of pleasure leave his vision going dark at the edges until the edges are all there is.

* * *

He wakes the next day groggy and confused, watching Piers through eyes he's too exhausted to open fully. Piers looks beautiful, like he's glowing in the sun shining through the window: he's entirely naked and gracefully smoking a cigarette, the sun landing on his shining white skin and also on the clouds of white smoke.

"S'a bad habit," he says out of habit, his words slurring. "It'll kill you."

Piers' laugh is beautiful, musical. It makes Jacob feel like he's been drenched in icy water.

"Time's it?" he asks, voice coming out in a clumsy, half-swallowed mumble.

"Oh, about five," says Piers. "PM."

"No," says Jacob, wanting to shake his head but finding himself too dead tired to try.

That can't be fucking right. They went upstairs when it wasn't even ten — he can't have been sleeping a whole seventeen hours and be so exhausted he can barely raise his head.

"So much energy, such strength," says Piers warmly: his voice is sticky sweet, and it reminds him of tree sap. It reminds him of the way tree sap slides down tree bark, the way ants get caught up in the slide, drowned in it so they can't even struggle. "And look, darling."

Jacob flicks his eyes — he can't move his head — to stare, uncomprehending, at the pot he'd brought with him, which is at Piers' feet in the sunlight: from amidst the dark soil, a tiny shoot of green is sprouting.

"It might even last," says Piers sweetly. "You won't."

Unable to hold his head up any longer, Jacob falls back onto the bed, and darkness takes him.

FIN.

The Lighthouse

Routine was the most important thing. He'd maintained the lighthouse for years upon years now, and had grown comfortable in his habits. It made things easier, simpler. The lighthouse was his life.

Mornings were simple. Before breakfast he would check the lighthouse, turn off the bulb as the morning sun grew brighter. From there it was simple bit of cleaning up, dusting the room and tidying.

They had a fancy set up in the engines below, a diesel set that powered the whole tower and had to be fed new oil everyday.

Breakfast was a simple affair. When he'd been a young man, just starting out working the lighthouse with a permanent sailing injury, he'd varied every day. He'd bought bacon, eggs, bread, had changed his meal — the wages were fairly decent, after all, and it wasn't hard to afford little variety, so long as he made the trip into town.

These days, it was very different. He had settled into taking unsweetened porridge every morning. He never really thought on the taste: he just put it in the pot, heated it, and sat at his table with his bowl and spoon.

After that, it was the check of the grounds outside the lighthouse. Picking rubbish off the two beaches, ensuring nothing had broken, ensuring the paths were clear. That took a good three hours or so.

Lunch. Again, something simple.

Some days he would go off and into town — he couldn't remember the last time he'd done that. Today was not one of those days. This day he would settle in his chair and listen to the radio.

His radio was old, but it worked fine. He'd listen to the news, listen to music. Sometimes there was a little static, but that never lasted too long.

From there, he would wait. When night came, he would pick up his radio and head upstairs to turn on the switches and then settle with the light. He would watch from the window and look for ships, for boats, even for little dinghies.

The lighthouse ran automatically for the most part, but he liked to be there. He liked to see. He'd done this for so many years now, after all.

Routine was important.

Sometimes he fell asleep, but he always woke in his bed on the next day. He must do it in some sleepy daze, he thought. Stagger half-awake to his bed and then forget about it by the time he woke.

It was part of the routine, the ever-important schedule. That's how it worked.

* * *

He'd heard about the lighthouse, but it had been left to nothingness for many years now. It was just a monument to past days on the outcrop of cliff, and had been mostly forgotten about.

Someone had mentioned preserving it, perhaps making a museum of sorts. Someone else had agreed to take the ancient keys and check it out.

He swung the keys in his hand as he stepped onto its little island from the bridge, following the path. It was overgrown, plants spanning out onto the yellowed line of it. The beach he could see was strewn over with cans and seaweed and plastic: that would have to be fixed and cleaned up.

The door to the lighthouse was thick and made of oak. The key stuck a little in the door, but he managed to turn the key and open it. As he stepped into the lighthouse, into the kitchen, he saw a silver shadow of something in the old chair at the table.

The ghost disappeared, routine forgotten, and he barely even noticed it.

His thoughts went to the old antique radio on the sideboard, and wondered if it should stay in the museum or not.

FIN.

The Shepherd

"Red sky at night, shepherd's delight."

It is late. It seems it has been late for a very long time — but then, is time stretched when one is lost? Are not all people lost, at one time or another? And when one is lost, does time pass slower, or has the warm summer sun truly been just below the horizon for hours upon hours, bathing the sky in its rosy hue?

No. Not rosy.

To be rosy is a pleasant thing, charming, calming — *la vie en rose* is to see all things as lovely. This dusk, this strange parody of evening time, it is not at all lovely. There is something wrong, some edge to the sky that causes discomfort.

It is warm, and the lingering heat from the day is pleasant, soaking into the bones and remaining there. Ah, so relaxing. The thought of sleep is impossible to suppress, as that lulling haze sinks over everything.

It is like the exquisite background hum that comes from a little good wine: yes, it is like intoxication.

But the sky is too red, too wrong, to sleep beneath it. It is not the dark blanket of night: it is something else, some odd purgatory that will not allow for sleeping nor waking — dreaming, perhaps. Perhaps this is all a dream. A beautiful dream soaked with red — but not a rosy red.

If that colour is not rosy, what is it instead? It is too light to be as autumn leaves, too dark to be as the soft pink of cherry blossom. The cherries themselves, perhaps, red with summer's sweet, sweet blood?

Blood. Yes, that is what that colour is akin to, decadent, inviting, with a promise of warmth — it is wrong.

It is so *very* wrong.

The path is well-used, and yet every step under this blood-red sky feels like a disturbance, as if the countryside about is hallowed ground.

A thin place, yes, where once a thousand years ago red, **red** sacrifices were made.

Stop.

There is a spatter of rich liquid on the ground, sinking slowly into the dirt of the path as if to sate its thirst for wine, but this cannot be wine — it is blood.

This is so very, very wrong.

A thousand years ago? Perhaps that was wishful thinking — *la vie en rose.* How long ago had those thoughts been? The sun hovers still, below the horizon, not yet sinking down completely and letting the rural land go dark. How long is this path? How many steps have been tread on its brown flesh?

The path must be continued: there is no other. To walk the golden fields and stray from the track when every crop is bathed in the sky's blood reflection seems wrong — the path is hallowed, but those fields are truly sacred, pure.

They must not be touched.

Each footstep is heavier than the last; a sleepy haze surrounds everything now, and even the field crops of barley seem to sway to it, as if these golden ears are tipsy too. But sleep would still be wrong — the lull, at least, creates a pleasant rhythm.

A heavy step. Another. Two more. Ten more. So many steps, one after the other, rhythmic, like the beat of some tired drum. Were drums once played here, long ago? How long will it be until drums are heard again?

The sky is still so very red — it has been too long now. Does the path go on forever? Maybe. Perhaps. Possibly.

More blood on the ground. It is fresh: it has not yet had time to seep into the dry, parched earth to be tasted. Strange, how sights so simple can cause the heart to speed, the lungs to expand, the chest to feel so strained, so tight, so tight, so-

There is a shepherd.

The shepherd wears a brown cloth, over the head, hiding the hair, shrouding the body — it is the same colour as the parched, thirsty ground. There is a silent imperative — walk to the shepherd. Kneel before the shepherd. Sleep at the shepherd's feet, and be at **peace**.

Let the shepherd's thirst be sated.

But the shepherd is in one of the fields, in the centre of a sacred, sacred plot of brown earth and golden crop — every strand of barley lies flat upon the ground, as if the shepherd had come from above and landed with such tremendous, divine force that all the crop had been thrust away.

Perhaps that is what happened, but the past is the past and the shepherd was the only witness. No one will ask the shepherd if that was so — this fact is certain.

A step from the path onto grass that is yellow. It is yellow for want of hydration that water is too thin to remedy. This thought is somehow calming, although it ought not be.

Another step.

Why is the field uncontained? There are no hedges betraying its edges. Perhaps there are no edges as there are no hedges for fledglings to roost in, and with no fledglings no pledges are necessary from farmers not to disturb the hedges, or the edges of the hedges. Light-headed. Airy. It is like wine.

Perhaps the golden, blood-bathed field goes on forever.

That is not a calming thought: infinity is, by its very nature, unsettling. The shepherd is infinite: this is certain fact. Where does this knowledge come from?

The shepherd beckons.

More steps. So many steps. They are like a drumbeat — no. There *is* a drumbeat, distant, rhythmic; every step is fitted to its loud, clear metre. The shepherd's face is visible now, for that hood has been drawn back.

The shepherd is *beautiful.* Dark skin, handsome brown eyes, such plump, *inviting* lips. Beautiful. Divine. Those lips undoubtedly taste as good as wine, and are as intoxicating, even by sight. In one hand, the hand that is held out in a gesture to move to the floor, the shepherd holds nothing, but the other holds a thin, shining blade, light with a plain curve.

A scythe for the harvest.

Knees to the floor. Worship. Prayer.

A bowed head. Fealty. Sacrifice.

The shepherd does not move, not yet. The pause is heavy with blood and heat and warmth and the sun is still not sinking further when it ought have, when it ought be deep into the night by now — so many hours walking, walking, and now the drum is beating and it is *louder,* pounding through the ear drums, reverberating in the chest cavity.

The shepherd's left hand raises, the hand with the blade clasped in dark fingers, and then it comes down with a whistle through the air.

Pain. Wet heat on the neck, heavy, gushing: the world goes dark.

Above those two bodies, the standing shepherd looking down with the beginning of a smile on those beautiful lips; the other slumped on the floor, still, bleeding, to the horizon, where the sun is beginning to rise, flooding the sky with sweet gold and washing the blood away.

The shepherd laughs, but then the thin place becomes a thick place again, the world becomes real: those bodies fade.

"Red sky at night, shepherd's delight, Red sky in the morning, shepherd's warning."

FIN.

More from the Author

If you'd like to seek out more of my work, *Heart of Stone* is a full-length novel set in the 18th century, and is a slowburn slice-of-life romance between a vampire and his secretary, the vampire ADHD and the secretary autistic. It has a lot of humour and domestic elements throughout.

My most recent release, *Powder and Feathers*, is a long-form contemporary dark romance with a great many fantasy elements, featuring a fucked-up dynamic between a Fallen angel and a depressed artist he begins stalking in the park.

If you're interested in perusing more novella-length pieces and short stories, I publish a huge variety of short stories that are available on a subscription model from Patreon[1] or as part of your Medium[2] subscription!

I normally publish at least one new piece a week, whether that's short stories, longer form short stories like this one, serial updates for my chaptered works, or non-fiction pieces like essays and analyses.

My name is Johannes T. Evans on both sites.

My website: www.JohannesTEvans.com[3]

My Twitter: @JohannesTEvans[4]

And finally, if you'd like to get regular email updates from me, with media recommendations, links to my most recently published work, and other little announcements, you <u>can sign up at www.buttondown.email/JohannesTEvans.</u>

---

1. https://www.patreon.com/JohannesEvans

2. https://johannestevans.medium.com/directory-of-work-6291c6e102b9

3. http://www.JohannesTEvans.com

4. https://twitter.com/johannestevans